The
Choir Invisible

James Lane Allen

The Choir Invisible

James Lane Allen

© 1st World Library – Literary Society, 2005
PO Box 2211
Fairfield, IA 52556
www.1stworldlibrary.org
First Edition

LCCN: 2004195639

Softcover ISBN: 1-4218-0460-3
Hardcover ISBN: 1-4218-0360-7
eBook ISBN: 1-4218-0560-X

Purchase *"The Choir Invisible"*
as a traditional bound book at:
www.1stWorldLibrary.org/purchase.asp?ISBN=1-4218-0460-3

1st World Library Literary Society is a nonprofit
organization dedicated to promoting literacy by:

- Creating a free internet library accessible from any
computer worldwide.
- Hosting writing competitions and offering book
publishing scholarships.

**Readers interested in supporting literacy
through sponsorship, donations or
membership please contact:
literacy@1stworldlibrary.org
Check us out at: www.1stworldlibrary.ORG
and start downloading free ebooks today.**

The Choir Invisible
contributed by Tim, Ed & Rodney
in support of
1st World Library Literary Society

I

"O may I join the choir invisible
Of those immortal dead who live again
In minds made better by their presence. . . . . .
feed pure love,
Beget the smiles that have no cruelty,
Be the sweet presence of a good diffused
And in diffusion evermore intense.
So shall I join the choir invisible
Whose music is the gladness of the world."

GEORGE ELIOT

THE middle of a fragrant afternoon of May in the green wilderness of Kentucky: the year 1795.

High overhead ridges of many-peaked cloud - the gleaming, wandering Alps of the blue ether; outstretched far below, the warming bosom of the earth, throbbing with the hope of maternity. Two spirits abroad in the air, encountering each other and passing into one: the spirit of scentless spring left by melting snows and the spirit of scented summer born with the earliest buds. The road through the forest one of those wagon-tracks that were being opened from the clearings of the settlers, and that wound along beneath trees of which those now seen in Kentucky are the unworthy survivors - oaks and walnuts, maples and elms, centuries old, gnarled, massive, drooping, majestic , through whose arches the sun hurled down only some solitary spear of gold, and over whose gray-mossed roots some cold brook crept in silence; with here and there billowy open spaces of wild rye, buffalo grass, and clover on which the light fell in sheets of radiance; with other spots so dim that for ages no shoot had sprung from the deep black mould; blown to and fro across this wagon-road, odours of ivy, pennyroyal and mint, mingled with the fragrance of the wild grape; flitting to and fro across it, as low as the violet-beds, as high as the sycamores, unnumbered kinds of birds, some of which like the paroquet are long since vanished.

Down it now there came in a drowsy amble an old white bob-tail horse, his polished coat shining like silver when he crossed an expanse of sunlight, fading into spectral paleness when he passed under the rayless trees; his foretop floating like a snowy plume in the light wind, his unshod feet, half-covered by the fetlocks, stepping noiselessly over the loamy earth; the rims of his nostrils expanding like flexible ebony; and in his eyes that look of peace which is never seen but in those of petted animals.

He had on an old bridle with knots of blue violets hanging, down at his ears; over his broad back was spread a blanket of buffalo-skin; on this rested a worn black side-saddle, and sitting in the saddle was a girl, whom every young man of the town not far away knew to be Amy Falconer, and whom many an old pioneer dreamed of when he fell asleep beside his rifle and his hunting-knife in his lonely cabin of the wilderness. She was perhaps the first beautiful girl of aristocratic birth ever seen in Kentucky, and the first of the famous train

of those who for a hundred years since have wrecked
or saved the lives of the men.

Her pink calico dress, newly starched and ironed, had
looked so pretty to her when she had started from
home, that she had not been able to bear the thought of
wearing over it this lovely afternoon her faded, mud-
stained riding-skirt; and it was so short that it showed,
resting against the saddle-skirt, her little feet loosely
fitted into new bronze morocco shoes. On her hands
she had drawn white half-hand mittens of home-knit;
and on her head she wore an enormous white scoop-
bonnet, lined with pink and tied under her chin in a
huge muslin bow. Her face, hidden away under the
pink-and-white shadow, showed such hints of pearl
and rose that it seemed carved from the inner surface
of a sea-shell. Her eyes were gray, almond shaped,
rather wide apart, with an expression changeful and
playful, but withal rather shrewd and hard; her light
brown hair, as fine as unspun silk, was parted over her
brow and drawn simply back behind her ears; and the
lips of her little mouth curved against each other, fresh,
velvet-like, smiling.

On she rode down the avenue of the primeval woods;
and Nature seemed arranged to salute her as some
imperial presence; with the waving of a hundred green
boughs above on each side; with a hundred floating
odours; with the swift play of nimble forms up and
down the boles of trees; and all the sweet confusion of
innumerable melodies.

Then one of those trifles happened that contain the
history of our lives, as a drop of dew draws into itself
the majesty and solemnity of the heavens.

From the pommel of the side-saddle there dangled a heavy roll of home-spun linen, which she was taking to town to her aunt's merchant as barter for queen's-ware pitchers; and behind this roll of linen, fastened to a ring under the seat of the saddle, was swung a bundle tied up in a large blue-and-white checked cotton neck-kerchief. Whenever she fidgeted in the saddle, or whenever the horse stumbled as he often did because he was clumsy and because the road was obstructed by stumps and roots, the string by which this bundle was tied slipped a little through the lossening knot and the bundle hung a little lower down. Just where the wagon-trail passed out into the broader public road leading from Lexington to Frankfort and the travelling began to be really good, the horse caught one of his forefeet against the loop of a root, was thrown violently forward, and the bundle slipped noiselessly from the saddle to the earth.

She did not see it. She indignantly gathered the reins more tightly in her hand, pushed back her bonnet, which now hung down over her eyes like the bill of a pelican, and applied her little switch of wild cherry to the horse's flank with such vehemence that a fly which was about to alight on that spot went to the other side. The old horse himself - he bore the peaceable name of William Penn - merely gave one of the comforting switches of his bob-tail with which he brushed away the thought of any small annoyance, and stopped a moment to nibble at the wayside cane mixed with purple blossoming peavine.

Out of the lengthening shadows of the woods the girl and the horse passed on toward the little town; and far behind them in the public road lay the lost bundle.

James Lane Allen

II

IN the open square on Cheapside in Lexington there is now a bronze statue of John Breckinridge. Not far from where it stands the pioneers a hundred years ago had built the first log school-house of the town.

Poor old school-house, long since become scattered ashes! Poor little backwoods academicians, driven in about sunrise, driven out toward dusk! Poor little tired backs with nothing to lean against! Poor little bare feet that could never reach the floor! Poor little droop-headed figures, so sleepy in the long summer days, so afraid to fall asleep! Long, long since, little children of the past, your backs have become straight enough, measured on the same cool bed; sooner or later your feet, wherever wandering, have found their resting-places in the soft earth; and all your drooping heads have gone to sleep on the same dreamless pillow and there are sleeping. And the young schoolmaster, who seemed exempt from frailty while he guarded like a sentinel that lone outpost of the alphabet - he too has long since joined the choir invisible of the immortal dead. But there is something left of him though more than a century has passed away: something that has wandered far down the course of time to us like the faint summer fragrance of a young tree long since fallen dead in its wintered forest - like a dim radiance yet travelling onward into space from an orb turned black and cold - like an old melody, surviving on and on in the air without any instrument, without any strings.

John Gray, the school-master. At four o'clock that afternoon and therefore earlier than usual, he was standing on the hickory block which formed the doorstep of the school-house, having just closed the door behind him for the day. Down at his side, between the thumb and forefinger of one hand, hung his big black hat, which was decorated with a tricoloured cockade, to show that he was a member of the Democratic Society of Lexington, modelled after the Democratic Society of Philadelphia and the Jacobin clubs of France. In the open palm of the other lay his big silver English lever watch with a glass case and broad black silk fob.

A young fellow of powerful build, lean, muscular; wearing simply but with gentlemanly care a suit of black, which was relieved around his wrists and neck by linen, snow-white and of the finest quality. In contrast with his dress, a complexion fresh, pure, brilliant - the complexion of health and innocence; in contrast with this complexion from above a mass of coarse dark-red hair, cut short and loosely curling. Much physical beauty in the head, the shape being noble, the pose full of dignity and of strength; almost no beauty in the face itself except in the gray eyes which were sincere, modest, grave. Yet a face not without moral loftiness and intellectual power; rugged as a rock, but as a rock is made less rugged by a little vine creeping over it, so his was softened by a fine network of nerves that wrought out upon it a look of kindness; betraying the first nature of passion, but disciplined to the higher nature of control; youthful,

James Lane Allen

but wearing those unmistakable marks of maturity which mean a fierce early struggle against the rougher forces of the world. On the whole, with the calm, self respecting air of one who, having thus far won in the battle of life, has a fiercer longing for larger conflict, and whose entire character rests on the noiseless conviction that he is a man and a gentleman.

Deeper insight would have been needed to discover how true and earnest a soul he was; how high a value he set on what the future had in store for him and on what his life would be worth to himself and to others; and how, liking rather to help himself than to be helped, he liked less to be trifled with and least of all to be seriously thwarted.

He was thinking, as his eyes rested on the watch, that if this were one of his ordinary days he would pursue his ordinary duties; he would go up street to the office of Marshall and for the next hour read as many pages of law as possible; then get his supper at his favourite tavern - the Sign of the Spinning, Wheel - near the two locust trees; then walk out into the country for an hour or more; then back to his room and more law until midnight by the light of his tallow dip.

But this was not an ordinary day - being one that he had long waited for and was destined never to forget. At dusk the evening before, the post-rider, so tired that he had scarce strength of wind to blow his horn, had ridden into town bringing the mail from Philadelphia; and in this mail there was great news for him. It had kept him awake nearly all of the night before; it had been uppermost in his mind the entire day in school. At the thought of it now he thrust his watch into his pocket, pulled his hat resolutely over his brow, and started toward Main Street, meaning to turn thence toward Cross Street, now known as Broadway. On the outskirts of the town in that direction lay the wilderness, undulating away for hundreds of miles like a vast green robe with scarce a rift of human making.

He failed to urge his way through the throng as speedily as he may have expected, being withheld at moments by passing acquaintances, and at others pausing of his own choice to watch some spectacle of the street.

The feeling lay fresh upon him this afternoon that not many years back the spot over which the town was spread had been but a hidden glade in the heart of the beautiful, awful wilderness, with a bountiful spring bubbling up out of the turf, and a stream winding away through the green, valley-bottom to the bright, shady Elkhorn: a glade that for ages had been thronged by stately-headed elk and heavy-headed bison, and therefore sought also by unreckoned generations of soft-footed, hard eyed red hunters. Then had come the beginning of the end when one summer day, toward sunset, a few tired, rugged backwoodsmen of the Anglo-Saxon race, wandering fearless and far into the wilderness from the eastern slopes of the Blue Ridge and the Alleghanies, had made their camp by the margin of the spring; and always afterwards, whether by day or by night, they had dreamed of this as the land they must conquer for their homes. Now they had conquered it already; and now this was the town that had been built there, with its wide streets under big trees of the primeval woods; with a long stretch of turf on one side of the stream for a town common; with inns and taverns in the style of those of country England or of Virginia in the reign of George the

Third; with shops displaying the costliest merchandise of Philadelphia; with rude dwellings of logs now giving way to others of frame and of brick; and, stretching away from the town toward the encompassing wilderness, orderly gardens and orchards now pink with the blossom of the peach, and fields of young maize and wheat and flax and hemp.

As the mighty stream of migration of the Anglo-Saxon race had burst through the jagged channels of the Alleghanies and rushed onward to the unknown, illimitable West, it was this little town that had received one of the main streams, whence it flowed more gently dispersed over the rich lands of the newly created State, or passed on to the Ohio and the southern fringes of the Lakes. It was this that received also a vast return current of the fearful, the disappointed, the weak, as they recoiled from the awful frontier of backwood life and resought the peaceful Atlantic seaboard - one of the defeated Anglo-Saxon armies of civilization.

These two far-clashing tides of the aroused, migrating race - the one flowing westward, the other ebbing eastward - John Gray found himself noting with deep interest as he moved through the town that afternoon a hundred years ago; and not less keenly the unlike groups and characters thrown dramatically together upon this crowded stage of border history.

At one point his attention was arrested by the tearful voices of women and the weeping of little children: a company of travellers with pack-horses - one of the caravans across the desert of the Western woods - was moving off to return by the Wilderness Road to the old abandoned homes in Virginia and North Carolina.

Farther on, his passage was blocked by a joyous crowd that had gathered about another caravan newly arrived - not one traveller having perished on the way. Seated on the roots of an oak were a group of young backwoodsmen - swarthy, lean, tall, wild and reckless of bearing - their long rifles propped against the tree or held fondly across the knees; the gray smoke of their pipes mingling with the gray of their jauntily worn raccoon-skin caps; the rifts of yellow sunlight blending with the yellow of their huntingshirts and tunics; their knives and powder-horns fastened in the belts that girt in their gaunt waists: the heroic youthful sinew of the old border folk. One among them, larger and handsomer than the others, had pleased his fancy by donning more nearly the Indian dress. His breech-clout was of dappled fawn-skin; his long thigh boots of thin deer-hide were open at the hips, leaving exposed the clear whiteness of his flesh; below the knees they were ornamented by a scarlet fringe tipped with the hoofs of fawns and the spurs of the wild turkey; and in his cap he wore the intertwined wings of the hawk and the scarlet tanager.

Under another tree in front of a tavern bearing the sign of the Virginia arms, a group of students of William and Mary, the new aristocrats of the West, were singing, gambling, drinking; while at intervals one of them, who had lying open before him a copy of Tom Paine's "Age of Reason," pounded on the table and apostrophied the liberties of Man. Once Gray paused beside a tall pole that had been planted at a street corner and surmounted with a liberty cap. Two young men, each wearing the tricolour cockade as he did, were standing, there engaged in secret conversation. As he joined them, three other young men - Federalists - sauntered past, wearing black cockades, with an eagle button on the left side. The six men saluted coolly.

Many another group and solitary figure he saw to remind him of the turbulent history of the time and place. A parson, who had been the calmest of Indian fighters, had lost all self-control as he contended out in the road with another parson for the use of Dr. Watts' hymns instead of the Psalms of David. Near by, listening to them, and with a wondering eye on all he saw in the street, stood a French priest of Bordeaux, an exile from the fury of the avenging jacobins. There were brown flatboatmen, in weather-beaten felt hats, just returned by the long overland trip from New Orleans and discussing with tobacco merchants the open navigation of the Mississippi; and as they talked, up to them hurried the inventor Edward West, who said with excitement that if they would but step across the common to the town branch, he would demonstrate by his own model that some day navigation would be by steam: whereat they all laughed kindly at him for a dreamer, and went to laugh at the action of his mimic boat, moving hither and thither over the dammed water of the stream. Sitting on a stump apart from every one, his dog at his feet, his rifle across his lap, an aged backwoodsman surveyed in sorrow the civilization that had already destroyed his hunting and that was about sending him farther west to the depths of Missouri - along with the buffalo. His glance fell with disgust upon two old gentlemen in knee-breeches who met and offered each other their snuff-boxes, with a deep bow. He looked much more kindly at a crave, proud Chickasaw hunter, who strode by with inward grief and shame, wounded by the robbery of his people. Puritans from New England; cavaliers from Virginia; Scotch-Irish from Pennsylvania; mild-eyed trappers and bargemen from the French hamlets of Kaskaskia and Cahokia; wood-choppers; scouts; surveyors; swaggering adventurers; land-lawyers; colonial burgesses, - all these mingled and jostled, plotted and bartered, in the shops, in the streets, under the trees.

And everywhere soldiers and officers of the Revolution - come West with their families to search for homes, or to take possession of the grants made them by the Government. In the course of a short walk John Gray passed men who had been wounded in the battle of Point Pleasant; men who had waded behind Clark through the freezing marshes of the Illinois to the storming of Vincennes; men who had charged through flame and smoke up the side of King's Mountain against Ferguson's Carolina loyalists; men who with chilled ardour had let themselves be led into the massacre of the Wabash by blundering St. Clair; men who with wild thrilling pulses had rushed to victory behind mad Antony Wayne.

And the women! Some - the terrible lioness-mothers of the Western jungles who had been used like men to fight with rifle, knife, and axe - now sat silent in the doorways of their rough cabins, wrinkled, scarred, fierce, silent, scornful of all advancing luxury and refinement. Flitting gaily past them, on their way to the dry goods stores - supplied by trains of pack-horses from over the Alleghanies, or by pack-horse and boat down the Ohio - hurried the wives of the officers, daintily choosing satins and ribands for a coming ball. All this and more he noted as he passed lingeringly on. The deep vibrations of history swept through him, arousing him as the marshalling storm cloud, the rush of winds, and sunlight flickering into gloom kindle the sense of the high, the mighty, the sublime.

As he was crossing the common, a number of young fellows stripped and girt for racing - for speed greater than an Indian's saved many a life in those days, and running was part of the regular training of the young - bounded up to him like deer, giving a challenge: he too was very swift. But he named another day, impatient of the many interruptions that had already delayed him, and with long, rapid strides he had soon passed beyond the last fields and ranges of the town. Then he slackened his pace. Before him, a living wall, rose the edge of the wilderness. Noting the position of the sun and searching for a point of least resistance, he plunged in.

Soon he had to make his way through a thicket of cane some twelve feet high; then through a jungle of wild rye, buffalo grass and briars; beyond which he struck a narrow deertrace and followed that in its westward winding through thinner undergrowth under the dark trees.

He was unarmed. He did not even wear a knife. But the thought rose in his mind of how rapidly the forest also was changing its character. The Indians were gone. Two years had passed since they had for the last time flecked the tender green with tender blood. And the deadly wild creatures - the native people of earth and tree - they likewise had fled from the slaughter and starvation of their kind. A little while back and a maddened buffalo or a wounded elk might have trodden him down and gored him to death in that thicket and no one have ever learned his fate - as happened to many a solitary hunter. He could not feel sure that hiding in the leaves of the branches against which his hat sometimes brushed there did not lie the panther, the hungrier for the fawns that had been driven from the near coverts. A swift lowering of its head, a tense noiseless spring, its fangs buried in his neck, - with no knife the contest would not have gone well with him. But of deadly big game he saw no sign that day. Once from a distant brake he was surprised to hear the gobble of the wild turkey; and more surprised still - and delighted - when the trail led to a twilight gloom and coolness, and at the green margin of a little spring he saw a stag drinking. It turned its terrified eyes upon him for an instant and then bounded away like a gray shadow.

When he had gone about two miles, keeping his face steadily toward the sun, he came upon evidences of a clearing: burnt and fallen timber; a field of sprouting maize; another of young wheat; a peach orchard flushing all the green around with its clouds of pink; beyond this a garden of vegetables; and yet farther on, a log house.

He was hurrying on toward the house; but as he passed the garden he saw standing in one corner, with a rake in her hand, a beautifully formed woman in homespun, and near by a negro lad dropping garden-seed. His eyes lighted up with pleasure; and changing his course at once, he approached and leaned on the picket fence.

"How do you do, Mrs. Falconer?"

She turned with a cry, dropping her rake and pushing her sun-bonnet back from her eyes.

"How unkind to frighten me!" she said, laughing as she recognized him; and then she came over to the fence and gave him her hand - beautiful, but hardened by work. A faint colour had spread over her face.

"I didn't mean to frighten you," he replied, smiling at her fondly. "But I had rapped on the fence twice. I suppose you took me for a flicker. Or you were too busy with your gardening to hear me. Or, may be you were too deep in your own thoughts."

"How do you happen to be out of school so early?" she asked, avoiding the subject.

"I was through with the lessons."

"You must have hurried."

"I did."

"And is that the way you treat people's children?"

"That's the way I treated them to-day."

"And then you came straight out here?"

"As straight and fast as my legs could carry me - with a good many interruptions."

She searched his face eagerly for a moment. Then her eyes fell and she turned back to the seed-planting. He stood leaning over the fence with his hat in his hand, glancing impatiently at the house.

"How can you respect yourself, to stand there idling and see me hard at work?" she said at length, without looking, at him.

"But you do the work so well - better than I could! Besides, you are obeying a Divine law. I have no right to keep you from doing the will of God. I observe you as one of the daughters of Eve - under the curse of toil."

"There's no Divine command that I should plant beans. But it is my command that Amy shall. And this is Amy's work. Aren't you willing to work for her?" she asked, slowly raising her eyes to his face.

"I am willing to work for her, but I am not willing to do her work!" he replied." If the queen sits quietly in the parlour, eating bread and honey" - and he nodded, protesting, toward the house.

"The queen's not in the parlour, eating bread and honey. She has gone to town to stay with Kitty Poythress till after the ball."

She noted how his expression instantly changed, and how, unconscious of his own action, he shifted his face back to the direction of the town.

"Her uncle was to take her in to-morrow," she went on, still watching him, "but no! she and Kitty must see each other to-night; and her uncle must be sure to bring her party finery in the gig to-morrow. I'm sorry you had your walk for nothing; but you'll stay to supper?"

"Thank you; I must go back presently."

"Didn't you expect to stay when you came?"

He flushed and laughed in confusion.

"If you'll stay, I'll make you a johnny-cake on a new ash shingle with my own hands."

"Thank you, I really must go back. But if there's a johnny-cake already made, I could easily take it along."

"My johnny-cakes do not bear transportation."

"I wouldn't transport it far, you know."

"Do stay! Major Falconer will be so disappointed. He said at dinner there were so many things he wanted to talk to you about. He has been looking for you to come out. And, then, we have had no news for weeks. The major has been too busy to go to town; and I! - I am as dry as one of the gourds of Confucius."

His thoughts settled contentedly upon her once more and his face cleared.

"I can't stay to supper, but I'll keep the Indians away till the major comes," he said. "What were you thinking of when I surprised you?"

"What was I thinking of?" She stopped working while she repeated his words and folded her hands about the handle of the rake as if to rest awhile. A band of her soft, shining hair, loosened by its own weight when she had bent over to thin some seed carelessly scattered in the furrow, now fell across her forehead. She pushed her bonnet back and stood gathering it a little absently into its place with the tips of her fingers. Meanwhile he could see that her eyes rested upon the edge of the wilderness. It seemed to him that she must be thinking of that; and he noted with pain, as often before, the contrast between her and her surroundings. From every direction the forest appeared to be rushing in upon that perilous little reef of a clearing - that unsheltered island of human life, newly displaying itself amid the ancient, blood-flecked, horror-haunted sea of woods. And shipwrecked on this island, tossed to it by one of the long tidal waves of history, there to remain in exile from the manners, the refinement, the ease, the society to which she had always been accustomed, this remarkable gentlewoman.

III

HE had learned a great deal about her past, and held it mirrored in his memory. The general picture of it rose before his eyes now, as he leaned on the fence this pleasant afternoon in May and watched her restoring to its place, with delicate strokes of her finger-tips, the lock of her soft, shining hair.How could any one so fine have thriven amid conditions so exhausting? Those hard toiling fingers, now grasping the heavy hoe, once used to tinkle over the spinet; the small, sensitive feet, now covered with coarse shoe-packs tied with leather thongs, once shone in rainbow hues of satin slippers and silken hose. A sunbonnet for the tiara of osprey plumes; a dress spun and woven by her own hand out of her own flax, instead of the stiff brocade; log hut for manor-house; one negro boy instead of troops of servants: to have possessed all that, to have been brought down to all this, and not to have been ruined by it, never to have lost distinction or been coarsened by coarseness never to have parted with grace of manner or grace of spirit, or been bent or broken or overclouded in character and ideals, - it was all this that made her in his eyes a great woman, a great lady.

He held her in such reverence that, as he caught the serious look in her eyes at his impulsive question, he was sorry he had asked it: the last thing he could ever have thought of doing would have been to intrude upon the privacy of her reflections.

"What was I thinking of?"

There was a short silence and then she turned to him eagerly, brightly, with an entire change of voice and expression - "But the news from town - you haven't told me the news." "Oh, there is any amount of news!" he cried, glad of a chance to retreat from his intrusion. And he began lightly, recklessly: "A bookbinder has opened a shop on Cross Street - a capital hand at the business, by the name of Leischman - and he will bind books at the regular market prices in exchange for linen rags, maple sugar, and goose-quills. I advise you to keep an eye on your geese, if the major once takes a notion to have his old Shakespeare and his other volumes, that had their bindings knocked off in crossing the Alleghanies, elegantly rebound. You can tell him also that after a squirrel-hunt in Bourbon County the farmers counted scalps, and they numbered five thousand five hundred and eighty-nine; so that he is not the only one who has trouble with his corn. And then you can tell him that on the common the other day Nelson Tapp and Willis Tandy had a fearful fight over a land-suit. Now it was Tandy and Tapp; now it was Tapp and Tandy; but they went off at last and drowned themselves and the memory of the suit in a bowl of sagamity.""And there is no news for me, I suppose?"

"Oh yes! I am happy to inform you that at McIllvain's you can now buy the finest Dutch and English letter-paper, gilt, embossed, or marbled."

"That is not very important; I have no correspondents." "Well, a saddlery has been opened by two fellows from

London, England, and you can now buy Amy a new side-saddle. She needs one." "Nor is that! The major buys the saddles for the family." "Well, then, as I came out on Alain Street, I passed some ladies who accused me of being on my way here, and who impressed it upon me that I must tell you of the last displays of women-wear: painted and velvet ribbons, I think they said, and crepe scarfs, and chintzes and nankeens and moreens and sarcenets, and - oh yes!-some muslinette jackets tamboured with gold and silver. They said we were becoming civilized - that the town would soon be as good as Williamsburg, or Annapolis, or Philadelphia for such things. You see I am like my children: I remember what I don't understand."

"I understand what I must not remember! Don't tell me of those things," she added. "They remind me of the past; they make me think of Virginia. I wear homespun now, and am a Kentuckian.""Well, then, the Indians fired on the Ohio packet-boat near Three Islands and killed - "

"Oh!" she said, with pain and terror, "don't tell me of that, either! It reminds me of the present.""Well, in Holland two thousand cats have been put into the corn-stores, to check the ravages of rats and mice," he said, laughing.

"What is the news from France? Do be serious!" "In New York some Frenchmen, seeing their flag insulted by Englishmen who took it down from the liberty-cap, went upstairs to the room of an English officer named Codd, seized his regimental coat and tore it to pieces."

"I'm glad of it! It was a very proper action!" "But, madam, the man Codd was perfectly innocent!" "No matter! His coat was guilty. They didn't tear him to pieces; they tore his coat. Are there any new books at the stores?"

"A great many! I have spent part of the last three days in looking over them. You can have new copies of your old favourites, Joseph Andrews, or Roderick Random, or Humphrey Clinker. You can have Goldsmith and Young, and Chesterfield and Addison. There is Don Quixote and Hudibras, Gulliver and Hume, Paley and Butler, Hervey and Watts, Lavater and Trenck, Seneca and Gregory, Nepos and even Aspasia Vindicated - to say nothing of Abelard and Heloise and Thomas a Kempis. All the Voltaires have been sold, however, and the Tom Paines went off at a rattling gait. By the way, while on the subject of books, tell the major that we have raised five hundred dollars toward buying books for the Transylvania Library, and that as soon as my school is out I am to go East as a purchasing committee. What particularly interests me is that I am going to Mount Vernon, to ask a subscription from President Washington. Think of that! Think of my presenting myself there with my tricoloured cockade - a Kentucky Jacobin!" "The President may be so occupied with the plots of you Kentucky jacobins," she said, "that he will not feel much like supplying you with more literature." Then she added, looking at him anxiously, " And so you are going away?"

"I'm going, and I'm glad I'm going. I have never set eyes on a great man. It makes my heart beat to think of it. I feel as a young Gaul might who was going to Rome to ask Caesar for gold with which to overthrow him. Seriously, it would be a dreadful thing for the country if a treaty should be ratified with England.

There is not a democratic society from Boston to Charleston that will not feel enraged with the President. You may be sure that every patriot in Kentucky will be outraged, and that the Governor will denounce it to the House."

"There is news from France, then - serious news?" "Much, much! The National Convention has agreed to carry into full effect the treaty of commerce between the two Republics, and the French and American flags have been united and suspended in the hall. The Dutch have declared the sovereignty of the French, and French and Dutch patriots have taken St. Martin's. The English have declared war against the Dutch and granted letters of marque and reprisals. There has been a complete change in the Spanish Ministry. There has been a treaty made between France and the Grand Duke of Tuscany. The French fleet is in the West Indies and has taken possession of Guadeloupe. All French emigrants in Switzerland have been ordered to remove ten leagues from the borders of France. A hundred and fifty thousand Austrians are hurrying down toward the Rhine, to be reinforced by fifty thousand more."

He had run over these items with the rapidity of one who has his eye on the map of the world, noting, the slightest change in the situation of affairs that could affect Kentucky; and she listened eagerly like one no less interested.

"But the treaty! The treaty! The open navigation of the Mississippi!" she cried impatiently. "The last news is that the treaty will certainly be concluded and the open navigation of the Mississippi assured to us forever. The major will load his flatboats, drift down to New

Orleans, sell those Spanish fops his tobacco for its weight in gems, buy a mustang to ride home on, and if not robbed and murdered by the land-pirates on the way, come back to you like an enormous bumblebee from a clover-field, his thighs literally packed with gold."

"I am so glad, so glad, so glad!"

He drew from his pockets a roll.

"Here are papers for two months back. And now I've something else to tell you. That is one of the things I came for"

As he said this, his manner, hitherto full of humour and vivacity, turned grave, and his voice, sinking to a lower tone, became charged with sweetness. It was the voice in which one refined and sincere soul confides to another refined and sincere soul the secret of some new happiness that has come to it.

But noticing the negro lad, who had paused in his work several paces off and stood watching them, he said to her:

"May I have a drink?"

She turned to the negro:"Go to the spring-house and bring some water."The lad moved away, smiling to himself and shaking his head.

"He has broken all my pitchers," she added. "To-day I had to send my last roll of linen to town by Amy to buy more queen's-ware. The moss will grow on the bucket before he gets back." When the boy was out of

James Lane Allen

hearing, she turned again to him:

"What is it? Tell me quickly."

"I have had news from Philadelphia. The case is at last decided in favour of the heirs, and I come at once into possession of my share. It may be eight or ten thousand dollars." His voice trembled a little despite himself.

She took his hands in hers with a warm, close pressure, and tears of joy sprang to her eyes. The whole of his bare, bleak life was known to her; its half-starved beginning; its early merciless buffeting; the upheaval of vast circumstance in the revolutionary history of the times by which he had again and again been thrown back upon his own undefended strength; and stealthily following him from place to place, always closing around him, always seeking to strangle him, or to poison him in some vital spot, that most silent, subtle serpent of life - Poverty. Knowing this, and knowing also the man he had become, she would in secret sometimes liken him to one of those rare unions of delicacy and hardihood which in the world of wild flowers Nature refuses to bring forth except from the cranny of a cold rock. Its home is the battle-field of black roaring tempests; the red lightnings play among its roots; all night seamless snow-drifts are woven around its heart; no bee ever rises to it from the valley below where the green spring is kneeling; no morning bird ever soars past it with observant song; but in due time, with unswerving obedience to a law of beauty unfolding from within, it sets forth its perfect leaves and strains its steadfast face toward the sun.

These paltry thousands! She realized that they would lift from him the burden of debts that he had assumed, and give him, without further waiting, the libertyof his powers and the opportunities of the world."God bless you!" She said with trembling lips. "It makes me happier than it does you. No one else in the whole world is as glad as I am."Silence fell upon them. Both were thinking, but in very different ways - of the changes that would now take place in his life.

"Do you know," he said at length, looking into her face with the quietest smile, that if this lawsuit had gone against me it would have been the first great defeat of my life? Sorely as I have struggled, I have yet to encounter that common myth of weak men, an insurmountable barrier. The imperfection of our lives - what is it but the imperfection of our planning and doing? Shattered ideals - what hand shatters them but one's own? I declare to you at this moment, standing here in the clear light of my own past, that I firmly believe I shall be what I will, that I shall have what I want, and that I shall now go on rearing the structure of my life, to the last detail, just as I have long planned it."She did not answer, but stood looking at him with a new pity in her eyes. After all, was he so young, so untaught by the world? Had a little prosperity already puffed him up? "There will be this difference, of course," he added. "Hitherto I have had to build slowly; henceforth there will be no delay, now that I am free to lay hold upon the material. But, my dear friend, I cannot bear to think of my life as a structure to be successfully reared without settling at once how it is to be lighted from within. And, therefore, I have come to speak to you about - the lamp." As he said this a solemn beauty flashed out upon his face. As though the outer curtain of his nature had been drawn up, she now gazed into the depths and confidences.

Her head dropped quickly on her bosom; and she drew slightly back, as though to escape pain or danger."You must know how long I have loved Amy," he continued in a tone of calmness. "I have not spoken sooner, because the circumstances of my life made it necessary for me to wait; and now I wish to ask her to become my wife, and I am here to beg your consent first."

For some time she did not answer. The slip of an elm grew beside the picket fence, and she stood passing her fingers over the topmost leaves, with her head lowered so that he could not see her face. At length she said in a voice he could hardly hear:

"I have feared for a long time that this would come; but I have never been able to get ready for it, and I am not ready now."

Neither spoke for some time longer; only his expression changed, and he looked over at her with a compassionate, amused gravity, as though he meant to be very patient with her opposition. On her part, she was thinking - Is it possible that the first use he will make of his new liberty is to forge the chain of a new slavery? Is this some weak spot now to be fully revealed in his character? Is this the drain in the bottom of the lake that will in the end bring its high, clear level down to mud and stagnant shallows and a swarm of stinging insects? At last she spoke, but with difficulty:"I have known for a year that you were interested in Amy. You could not have been here so much without our seeing that. But let me ask you one question: Have you ever thought that I wished you to marry her?" "I have always beheld in you an unmasked enemy," he replied, smiling.

"Then I can go on," she said. "But I feel as though never in my life have I done a thing that is as near being familiar and unwomanly. Nevertheless, for your sake - for hers - for ours - it is my plain, hard duty to ask you whether you are sure - even if you should have her consent - that my niece is the woman you ought to marry." And she lifted to him her clear, calm eyes, prematurely old in the experience of life.

"I am sure," he answered with the readiness of one who has foreseen the question.

The negro boy approached with a bucket of cold crystal water, and he drank a big gourd full of it gratefully.

"You can go and kindle the fire in the kitchen," she said to the negro. "It is nearly time to be getting supper. I will be in by and by."

"You have been with her so much!" she continued to Gray after another interval of embarrassment. "And you know, or you ought to know, her disposition, her tastes, her ways and views of life. Is she the companion you need now? will always need?"

"I have been much with her," he replied, taking up her words with humorous gravity. "But I have never studied her as I have studied law. I have never cross-examined her for a witness, or prosecuted her as an attorney, or pronounced sentence on her is a judge. I am her advocate - and I am ready to defend her now - even to you!" "John! - ""I love her - that is all there is of it!"

"Suppose you wait a little longer."

"I have waited too long already from necessity." It was on his lips to add: "I have gone too far with her; it is too late to retreat;" but he checked himself.

"If I should feel, then, that I must withhold my consent?"

He grew serious, and after the silence of a few moments, he said with great respect:"I should be sorry; but - " and then he forbore.

"If Major Falconer should withhold his?" He shook his head, and set his lips, turning his face away through courtesy. "It would make no difference! Nothing would make any difference!" and then another silence followed. "I suppose all this would be considered the proof that you loved her," she began at length, despairingly, "but even love is not enough to begin with; much less is it enough to live by."

"You don't appreciate her! You don't do her justice!" he cried rudely. "But perhaps no woman can ever understand why a man loves any other woman!" "I am not thinking of why you love my niece," she replied, with a curl of pride in her nostril and a flash of anger in her eyes. "I am thinking of why you will cease to love her, and why you will both be unhappy if you marry her. It is not my duty to analyze your affections; it is my duty to take care of her welfare.""My dear friend," he cried, his face aglow with impatient enthusiasm - "my dear friend" and he suddenly lifted her hand to his lips, "I have but one anxiety in the whole matter: will you cease to be my friend if I act in opposition to your wishes?" "Should I cease to be your friend because you had made a mistake? It is not to me you are unkind," she answered, quickly withdrawing her hand.

Spots of the palest rose appeared on her cheeks, and she bent over and picked up the rake, and began to work.

"I must be going," he said awkwardly; "it is getting late."

"Yes," she said; "it is getting late."

Still he lingered, swinging his hat in his hand, ill at case, with his face set hard away. "Is that all you have to say to me?" he asked at length, wheeling and looking her steadily and fondly in the eyes.

"That is all," she replied, controlling the quiver in her voice; but then letting herself go a little, she added with slow distinctness: "You might remember this: some women in marrying demand all and give all: with good men they are the happy; with base men they are the brokenhearted. Some demand everything and give little: with weak men they are tyrants; with strong men they are the divorced. Some demand little and give all: with congenial souls they are already in heaven; with uncongenial they are soon in their graves. Some give little and demand little: they are the heartless, and they bring neither the joy of life nor the peace of death." "And which of these is Amy?" he said, after a minute of reflection. "And which of the men am I?" "Don't ask her to marry you until you find out both," she answered.

She watched him as he strode away from her across the clearing, with a look in her eyes that she knew nothing of - watched him, motionless, until his tall, black figure passed from sight behind the green sunlit wall of the wilderness. What undisciplined, unawakened strength there was in him! How far such a stride as that would carry him on in life! It was like the tread of one of his own forefathers in Cromwell's unconquer-able, hymn-singing armies. She loved to think of him as holding his descent from a line so pious and so grim: it served to account to her for the quality of stern, spiritual soldiership that still seemed to be the mastering trait of his nature. How long would it remain so, was the question that she had often asked of herself. A fighter in the world he would always be - she felt sure of that; nor was it necessary to look into his past to obtain this assurance; one had but to look into his eyes. Moreover, she had little doubt that with a temper so steadily bent on conflict, he would never suffer defeat where his own utmost strength was all that was needed to conquer. But as he grew older, and the world in part conquered him as it conquers so many of us, would he go into his later battles as he had entered his earlier ones - to the measure of a sacred chant? Beneath the sweat and wounds of all his victories would he carry the white lustre of conscience, burning untarnished in him to the end?

It was this religious purity of his nature and his life, resting upon him as a mantle visible to all eyes but invisible to him, that had, as she believed, attracted her to him so powerfully. On that uncouth border of Western civilization, to which they had both been cast, he was a little lonely in his way, she in hers; and this fact had drawn them somewhat together. He was a scholar, she a reader; that too had formed a bond. He had been much at their home as lover of her niece, and this intimacy had given her a good chance to take his wearing measure as a man. But over and above all other things, it was the effect of the unfallen in him, of the highest keeping itself above assault, of his first youth never yet brushed away as a bloom, that constituted to her his distinction among the men that she had known. It served to place him in contrast with the colonial Virginia society of her remembrance - a society in which even the minds of the clergy were not like a lawn scentless with the dew on it, but like a lawn parched by the afternoon sun and full of hot odours. It kept him aloof from the loose ways of the young backwoodsmen and aristocrats of the town, with whom otherwise he closely mingled. It gave her the right, she thought, to indulge a friendship for him such as she had never felt for any other man; and in this friendship it made it easier for her to overlook a great deal that was rude in him, headstrong, overbearing.

When, this afternoon, he had asked her what she was thinking of when he surprised her with his visit, she had not replied: she could not have avowed even to herself that she was thinking of such things as these: that having, for some years, drawn out a hard, dull life in that settlement of pathfinders, trappers, wood-choppers, hunters, Indian fighters, surveyors; having afterwards, with little interest, watched them, one by one, as the earliest types of civilization followed, - the merchant, the lawyer, the priest, the preacher of the Gospel, the soldiers and officers of the Revolution, - at last, through all the wilderness, as it now fondly seemed to her, she saw shining the white light of his long absent figure, bringing a new melody to the woods, a new meaning to her life, and putting an end to all her desire ever to return to the old society beyond the mountains.

His figure passed out of sight, and she turned and walked sorrowfully to the cabin, from the low rugged chimney of which a pale blue smoke now rose into the twilight air. She chid herself that she had confronted the declaration of his purpose to marry her niece with so little spirit, such faulty tact. She had long known that he would ask this; she had long gotten ready what she would say; but in the struggle between their wills, she had been unaccountably embarrassed, she had blundered, and he had left rather strengthened than weakened in his determination.

But she must prevent the marriage; her mind was more resolute than ever as to that. Slowly she reached the doorstep of the cabin, a roughly hewn log, and turning, stood there with her bonnet in her hand, her white figure outlined before the doorway, slender and still. The sun had set. Night was rushing on over the awful land. The wolf-dog, in his kennel behind the house, rose, shook himself at his chain, and uttered a long howl that reached away to the dark woods - the darker for the vast pulsing yellow light that waved behind them in the west like a gorgeous soft aerial fan. As the echoes died out from the peach orchard came the song of a robin, calling for love and rest. Then from another direction across the clearing another sound reached her: the careless whistle of the major, returning from his day's work in the field. When she heard that, her face took on the expression that a woman sometimes comes to wear when she has accepted what life has brought her although it has brought her nothing for which she cares; and her lips opened with an unconscious sigh of weariness - the weariness that has been gathering weariness for years and that runs on in weariness through the future.

Later, she was kneeling before the red logs of the fireplace with one hand shielding her delicate face from the blistering heat; in the other holding the shingle on which richly made and carefully shaped was the bread of Indian maize that he liked. She did not rise until she had placed it where it would be perfectly browned; otherwise he would have been disappointed and the evening would have been spoiled.

IV

JOHN GRAY did not return to town by his straight course through the forest, but followed the winding wagon-road at a slow, meditative gait. He was always thoughtful after he had been with Mrs. Falconer; he was unusually thoughtful now; and the gathering hush of night, the holy expectancy of stars, a flock of white clouds lying at rest low on the green sky like sheep in some far uplifted meadow, the freshness of the woods soon to be hung with dew, - all these melted into his mood as notes from many instruments blend in the ear. But he was soon aroused in an unexpected way. When he reached the place where the wagon-road passed out into the broader public road leading from Lexington to Frankfort, he came near stumbling over a large, loose bundle, tied in a blue and white neckerchief. Plainly it had been lost and plainly it was his duty to discover if possible to whom it belonged. He carried it to one side of the road and began to examine its contents: a wide, white lace tucker, two fine cambric handkerchiefs, two pairs of India cotton hose, two pairs of silk hose, two thin muslin handkerchiefs, a pair of long kid gloves, - straw colour, - a pair of white kid shoes, a pale-blue silk coat, a thin, white striped muslin dress.The articles were not marked. Whose could they be? Not Amy's: Mrs. Falconer had expressly said that the major was to bring her finery to town in the gig the next day. They might have been dropped by some girl or by some family servant, riding into town; he knew several young ladies, to any one of whom they might belong. He would inquire in the morning; and meantime, he would leave the bundle at the office of the printer, where lost articles were commonly kept until they could be advertised in the paper, and called for by their owners. He replaced the things, and carefully retied the ends of the kerchief. It was dark when he reached town, and he went straight to his room and locked the bundle in his closet. Then he hurried to his tavern, where his supper had to be especially cooked for him, it being past the early hour of the pioneer evening meal. While he sat out under the tree at the door, waiting and impatiently thinking that he would go to see Amy as soon as he could despatch it, the tavern-keeper came out to say that some members of the Democratic Society had been looking for him. Later on, these returned. A meeting of the Society had been called for that night, to consider news brought by the postrider the day previous and to prepare advices for the Philadelphia Society against the postrider's return: as secretary, he was wanted at the proceedings. He begged hard to be excused, but he was the scholar, the scribe; no one would take his place. When the meeting ended, the hour was past for seeing Amy. He went to his room and read law with flickering concentration of mind till near midnight. Then he snuffed out his candle, undressed, and stretched himself along the edge of his bed.

It was hard and coarse. The room itself was the single one that formed the ruder sort of pioneer cabin. The floor was the earth itself, covered here and there with the skins of wild animals; the walls but logs, poorly plastered. From a row of pegs driven into one of these hung his clothes - not many. The antlers of a stag over

James Lane Allen

the doorway held his rifle, his hunting-belt, and his hat. A swinging shelf displayed a few books, being eagerly added to as he could bitterly afford it - with a copy of Paley, lent by the Reverend James Moore, the dreamy, saintlike, flute-playing Episcopal parson of the town. In the middle of the room a round table of his own vigorous carpentry stood on a panther skin; and on this lay some copy books in which he had just set new copies for his children; a handful of goosequills to be fashioned into pens for them; the proceedings of the Democratic Society, freshly added to this evening; copies of the Kentucky Gazette containing essays by the political leaders of the day on the separation of Kentucky from the Union and the opening of the Mississippi to its growing commerce - among them some of his own, stately and academic, signed "Cato the Younger." Lying open on the table lay his Bible; after law, he always read a little in that; and to-night he had reread one of his favourite chapters of St.Paul: that wherein the great, calm, victorious soldier of the spirit surveys the history of his trials, imprisonments, beatings. In one corner was set a three-cornered cupboard containing his underwear, his new cossack boots, and a few precious things that had been his mother's: her teacup and saucer, her prayer-book. It was in this closet that he had put the lost bundle.

He had hardly stretched himself along the edge of his bed before he began to think of this. Every complete man embraces some of the qualities of a woman, for Nature does not mean that sex shall be more than a partial separation of one common humanity; otherwise we should be too much divided to be companionable. And it is these womanly qualities that not only endow a man with his insight into the other sex, but that enable him to bestow a certain feminine supervision upon his own affairs when no actual female has them in charge. If he marries, this inner helpmeet behaves in unlike ways toward the newly reigning usurper; sometimes giving up peaceably, at others remaining her life-long critic - reluctant but irremovable. If many a wife did but realize that she is perpetually observed not only by the eyes of a pardoning husband but by the eyes of another woman hidden away in the depths of his being, she would do many things differently and not do some things at all.

The invisible slip of a woman in Gray now began to question him regarding the bundle. Would not those delicate, beautiful things be ruined, thus put away in his closet? He got up, took the bundle out, laid it on his table, untied the kerchief, lifted carefully off the white muslin dress and the blue silk coat, and started with them toward two empty pegs on the wall. He never closed the door of his cabin if the night was fine. It stood open now and a light wind blew the soft fabrics against his body and limbs, so that they seemed to fold themselves about him, to cling to him. He disengaged them reluctantly - apologetically.

Then he lay down again. But now the dress on the wall fascinated him. The moonlight bathed it, the wind swayed it. This was the first time that a woman's garments had ever hung in his room. He welcomed the mere accident of their presence as though it possessed a forerunning intelligence, as though it were the annunciation of his approaching change of life. And so laughing to himself, and under the spell of a growing fancy, he got up again and took the little white shoes and set them on the table in the moonlight - on the open Bible and the speech of St.Paul - and then went back, and lay looking at them and dreaming - looking at them and dreaming.

His thoughts passed meantime like a shining flock of white doves to Amy, hovering about her. They stole onward to the time when she would be his wife; when lying thus, he would wake in the night and see her dress on the wall and feel her head on his bosom; when her little shoes might stand on his open Bible, if they chose, and the satin instep of her bare foot be folded in the hard hollow of his.

He uttered a deep, voiceless, impassioned outcry that she might not die young nor he die young; that the struggles and hardships of life, now seeming to be ended, might never begirt him or her so closely again; that they might grow peacefully old together. To-morrow then, he would see her; no, not tomorrow; it was long past midnight now. He got down on his bare knees beside the bed with his face buried in his hands and said his prayers.

And then lying outstretched with his head resting on his folded hands, the moonlight streaming through the window and lighting up his dark-red curls and falling on his face and neck and chest, the cool south wind blowing down his warm limbs, his eyes opening and closing in religious purity on the dress, and his mind opening and closing on the visions of his future, he fell asleep.

V

WHEN he awoke late, he stretched his big arms drowsily out before his face with a gesture like that of a swimmer parting the water: he was in truth making his way out of a fathomless, moonlit sea of dreams to the shores of reality. Broad daylight startled him with its sheer blinding revelation of the material world, as the foot of a swimmer, long used to the yielding pavements of the ocean, touches with surprise the first rock and sand.

He sprang up, bathed, dressed, and stepped out into the crystalline freshness of the morning. He was glowing with his exercise, at peace with himself and with all men, and so strong in the exuberance of his manhood that he felt he could have leaped over into the east, shouldered the sun, and run gaily, impatiently, with it up the sky. How could he wait to see Amy until it went up its long slow way and then down again to its setting? A powerful young lion may some time have appeared thus at daybreak on the edge of a jungle and measured the stretches of sand to be crossed before he could reach an oasis where memory told him was the lurking-place of love.

It was still early. The first smoke curled upward from the chimneys of the town; the melodious tinkle of bells reached his ear as the cows passed from the milking to the outlying ranges deep in their wild verdure. Even as he stood surveying the scene, along the path which ran close to his cabin came a bare-headed, nutbrown pioneer girl, whose close-fitting dress of white home-spun revealed the rounded outlines of her figure. She had gathered up the skirt which was short, to keep it from the tops of the wet weeds. Her bare, beautiful feet were pink with the cold dew. Forgotten, her slow fat cows had passed on far ahead; for at her side, wooing her with drooping lashes while the earth was still flushed with the morn, strolled a young Indian fighter, swarthy, lean tall, wild. His long thigh boots of thin deer-hide, open at the hips, were ornamented with a scarlet fringe and rattled musically with the hoofs of fawns and the spurs of the wild turkey; his gray racoonskin cap was adorned with the wings of the hawk and the scarlet tanager.

The magnificent young, warrior lifted his cap to the school-master with a quiet laugh; and the girl smiled at him and shook a warning finger to remind him he was not to betray them. He smiled back with a deprecating gesture to signify that he could be trusted. He would have liked it better if he could have said more plainly that he too had the same occupation now; and as he gazed after them, lingering along the path side by side, the long-stifled cravings of his heart rose to his unworldly, passionate eyes: he all but wished that Amy also milked the cows at early morning and drove them out to pasture.

When he went to his breakfast at the tavern, one of the young Williamsburg aristocrats was already there, pretending to eat; and hovering about the table, brisk to appease his demands, the daughter of the taverner: she as ruddy as a hollyhock and gaily flaunting her head from side to side with the pleasure of denying him everything but his food, yet meaning to kiss him when twilight came - once, and then to run.

Truly, it seemed that this day was to be given up to much pairing: as be thought it rightly should be and that without delay. When he took his seat in the school-room and looked out upon the children, they had never seemed so small, so pitiful. It struck him that Nature is cruel not to fit us for love and marriage as soon as we are born - cruel to make us wait twenty or thirty years before she lets us really begin to live. He looked with eyes more full of pity than usual at blear-eyed, delicate little Jennie, as to whom he could never tell whether it was the multiplication-table that made her deathly sick, or sickness that kept her from multiplying. His eye lit upon a wee, chubby-cheeked urchin on the end of a high, hard bench, and he fell to counting how many ages must pass before that unsuspicious grub would grow his palpitating wings of flame. He felt like making them a little speech and telling them how happy he was, and how happy they would all be when they got old enough to deserve it.

And as for the lessons that day, what difference could it make whether ideas sprouted or did not sprout in those useless brains? He answered all the hard questions himself; and, indeed, so sunny and exhila-rating was the weather of his discipline that little Jennie, seeing how the rays fell and the wind lay, gave up the multiplication-table altogether and fell to drawing tomahawks.

A remarkable mixture of human life there was in Gray's school. There were the native little Kentu-ckians, born in the wilderness - the first wild, hardy generation of the new people; and there were little folks from Virginia, from Tennessee, from North Carolina, and from Pennsylvania and other sources, huddled together, some uncouth, some gentle-born, and all starting out to be formed into the men and women of Kentucky. They had their strange, sad, heroic games and pastimes under his guidance. Two little girls would be driving the cows home about dusk; three little boys would play Indian and capture them and carry them off; the husbands of the little girls would form a party to the rescue; the prisoners would drop pieces of their dresses along the way; and then at a certain point of the woods - it being the dead of night now and the little girls being bound to a tree, and the Indians having fallen asleep beside their smouldering campfires - the rescuers would rush in and there would be whoops and shrieks and the taking of scalps and a happy return. Or some settlers would be shut up in their fort. The only water to be had was from a spring outside the walls, and around this the enemy skulked in the corn and grass. But their husbands and sweethearts must not perish of thirst. So, with a prayer, a tear, a final embrace, the little women marched out through the gates to the spring in the very teeth of death and brought back water in their wooden dinner-buckets. Or, when the boys would become men with contests of running and pitching quoits and wrestling, the girls would play wives and have a quilting, in a house of green alder-bushes, or be capped and wrinkled grandmothers sitting beside imaginary spinning-wheels and smoking imaginary pipes.

Sometimes it was not Indian warfare but civil strife. One morning as many as three Daniel Boones appeared on the playground at the same moment; and at once there was a dreadful fight to ascertain which was the genuine Daniel. This being decided, the spurious Daniels submitted to be: the one, Simon Kenton; the other, General George Rogers Clark.

And there was another game of history - more practical in its bearings - which he had not taught them, but which they had taught him; they had played it with him that very morning. When he had stepped across the open to the school, he found that the older boys, having formed themselves into a garrison for the defence of the smaller boys and girls, had barricaded the door and barred and manned the wooden windows: the schoolhouse had suddenly become a frontier station; they were the pioneers; he was the invading Indians - let him attack them if he dared! He did dare and that at once; for he knew that otherwise there would be no school that day or as long as the white race on the inside remained unconquered. So had ensued a rough-and-tumble scrimmage for fifteen minutes, during which the babies within wailed aloud with real terror of the battle, and he received some real knocks and whacks and punches through the loop-holes of the stockade: the end being arrived at when the schoolhouse door, by a terrible wrench from the outside, was torn entirely off its wooden hinges; and the victory being attributed - as an Indian victory always was in those days - to the overwhelming numbers of the enemy.

With such an opening of the day, the academic influence over childhood may soon be restored to forcible supremacy but will awaken little zest. Gray was glad therefore on all accounts that this happened to be the day on which he had promised to tell them of the battle of the Blue Licks. Thirteen years before and forty miles away that most dreadful of all massacres had taken place; and in the town were many mothers who still wept for their sons, many widows who still dreamed of their young husbands, fallen that beautiful, fatal August day beneath the oaks and the cedars, or floating down the red-dyed river. All the morning he could see the expectation of this story in their faces: a pair of distant, clearest eyes would be furtively lifted to his, then quickly dropped; or another pair more steadily directed at him through the backwoods loop-hole of two stockade fingers.

At noon, then, having dismissed the smaller ones for their big recess, he was standing amid the eager upturned faces of the others - bareheaded under the brilliant sky of May. He had chosen the bank of the Town Fork, where it crossed the common, as a place in which he should be freest from interruption and best able to make his description of the battle-field well understood. This stream flows unseen beneath the streets of the city now with scarce rent enough to wash out its grimy channel; but then it flashed broad and clear through the long valley of scattered cabins and orchards and cornfields and patches of cane.

It was a hazardous experiment with the rough jewels of those little minds. They were still rather like diamonds rolling about on the bottom of barbarian rivers than steadily set and mounted for the uses of civilization.

He fixed his eyes upon a lad in his fifteenth year, the commandant of the fort of the morning, who now stood at the water edge, watching him with breathless attention. A brave, sunny face; - a big shaggy head holding a mind in it as clear as a sphere of rock-crystal; already heated with vast ambition - a leader in the school, afterwards to be a leader in the nation -

Richard Johnson.

"Listen!" he cried; and when he spoke in, that tone he reduced everything turbulent to peace. "I have brought you here to tell you of the battle of the Blue Licks not because it was the last time, as you know, that an Indian army ever invaded Kentucky; not because a hundred years from now or a thousand years from now other school-boys and other teachers will be talking of it still; not because the Kentuckians will some day assemble on the field and set up a monument to their forefathers, your fathers and brothers; but because there is a lesson in it for you to learn now while you are children. A few years more and some of you boys will be old enough to fight for Kentucky or for your country. Some of you will be common soldiers who will have to obey the orders of your generals; some of you may be generals with soldiers under you at the mercy of your commands. It may be worth your own lives, it may save the lives of your soldiers, to heed this lesson now and to remember it then. And all of you - whether you go into battles of that sort or not - will have others; for the world has many kinds of fighting to be done in it and each of you will have to do his share. And whatever that share may be, you will need the same character, the same virtues, to encounter it victorious; for all battles are won in the same way, all conquerors are alike. This lesson, then, will help each of you to win, none of you to lose.

"Do you know what it was that brought about the awful massacre of the Blue Licks? It was the folly of one officer.

"Let the creek here be the Licking River. The Kentuckians, some on foot and some on horse, but all tired and disordered and hurrying along, had just reached the bank. Over on the other side - some distance back - the Indians were hiding in the woods and waiting. No one knew exactly where they were; every one knew they counted from seven hundred to a thousand. The Kentuckians were a hundred and eighty-two. There was Boone with the famous Boonsborough men, the very name of whom was a terror; there was Trigg with men just as good from Harrodsburg; there was Todd, as good as either, with the men from Lexington. More than a fourth of the whole were commissioned officers, and more fearless men never faced an enemy. There was but one among them whose courage had ever been doubted, and do you know what that man did? "After the Kentuckians had crossed the river to attack, been overpowered, forced back to the river again, and were being shot down or cut down in the water like helpless cattle, that man - his name was Benjamin Netherland - did this: He was finely mounted. He had quickly recrossed the river and had before him the open buffalo trace leading back home. About twenty other men had crossed as quickly as he and were urging their horses toward this road. But Netherland, having reached the opposite bank, wheeled his horse's head toward the front of the battle, shouted and rallied the others, and sitting there in full view and easy reach of the Indian army across the narrow river, poured his volley into the foremost of the pursuers, who were cutting down the Kentuckians in the river. He covered their retreat. He saved their lives.

"There was another soldier among them named Aaron Reynolds. He had had a quarrel some days before with Colonel Patterson and there was bad blood between them. During the retreat, he was galloping toward the ford. The Indians were close behind. But as he ran, he came upon Colonel Patterson, who had been wounded and, now exhausted, had fallen behind his comrades. Reynolds sprang from his horse, helped the officer to mount, saw him escape, and took his poor chance on foot. For this he fell into the hands of the Indians.

"That is the kind of men of whom that little army of a hundred and eighty-two was made up - the oak forest of Kentucky. "And yet, when they had reached the river in this pursuit and some twenty of the officers had come out before the ranks to hold a council of war and the wisest and the oldest were urging caution or delay, one of them - McGary - suddenly waved his hat in the air, spurred his horse into the river, and shouted:

"'Let all who are not cowards follow me!'

"They all followed; and then followed also the shame of defeat, the awful massacre, the sorrow that lasts among us still, and the loss to Kentucky of many a gallant young life that had helped to shape her destiny in the nation.

"Some day perhaps some historian will write it down that the Kentuckians followed McGary because no man among them could endure such a taunt. Do not believe him. No man among them even thought of the taunt: it had no meaning. They followed him because they were too loyal to desert him and those who went with him in his folly. Your fathers always stood together and fought together as one man, or Kentucky would never have been conquered; and in no battle of all the many that they ever fought did they ever leave a comrade to perish because he had made a mistake or was in the wrong.

"This, then, is your lesson from the battle of Blue Licks: Never go into a battle merely to show that you are not a coward: that of itself shows what a coward you are.

"Do not misunderstand me! whether you be men or women, you will never do anything in the world without courage. It is the greatest quality of the mind - next to honor. It is your king. But the king must always have a good cause. Many a good king has perished in a bad one; and this noblest virtue of courage has perhaps ruined more of us than any other that we possess. You know what character the old kings used always to have at their courts. I have told you a great deal about him. It was the Fool. Do you know what personage it is that Courage, the King, is so apt to have in the Court of the Mind? It is the Fool also. Lay these words away; you will understand them better when you are older and you will need to understand them very well. Then also you will know what I mean when I say to you this morning that the battle of the Blue Licks was the work of the Fool, jesting with the King."

He had gone to the field himself one Saturday not long before, walking thoughtfully over it. He had had with him two of the Lexington militia who, in the battle, had been near poor Todd, their colonel, while fighting like a lion to the last and bleeding from many wounds. The recollection of it all was very clear now, very poignant: the bright winding river, there broadening at its ford; the wild and lonely aspect of the country round about. On the farther bank the long lofty ridge of rock, trodden and licked bare of vegetation for ages by the countless passing buffalo; blackened by rain and sun; only the more desolate for a few dwarfish cedars and other timber scant and dreary to the eye.

Encircling this hill in somewhat the shape of a horseshoe, a deep ravine heavily wooded and rank with grass and underbrush. The Kentuckians, disorderly foot and horse, rushing in foolhardiness to the top of this uncovered expanse of rock; the Indians, twice, thrice, their number, engirdling its base, ringing them round with hidden death. The whole tragedy repossessed his imagination and his emotions. His face had grown pale, his voice took the measure and cadence of an old-time minstrel's chant, his nervous fingers should have been able to reach out and strike the chords of a harp. With uplifted finger he was going on to impress them with another lesson: that in the battles which would be sure to await them, they must be warned by this error of their fathers never to be over-hasty or over-confident, never to go forward without knowing the nature of the ground they were to tread, or throw themselves into a struggle without measuring the force of the enemy. He was doing this when a child came skipping joyously across the common, and pushing her way up to him through the circle of his listeners, handed him a note. He read it, and in an instant the great battle, hills, river, horse, rider, shrieks, groans, all vanished from his mind as silently as a puff of white smoke from a distant cannon.

For a while he stood with his eyes fixed upon the paper, so absorbed as not to note the surprise that had fallen upon the children. At length merely saying, "I shall have to tell you the rest some other day," he walked rapidly across the common in the direction from which the little messenger had come.

A few minutes later he stood at the door of Father Poythress, the Methodist minister, asking for Amy. But she and Kitty had ridden away and would not return till night. Leaving word that he would come to see her in the evening, he turned away.

The children were scattered: there could be no more of the battle that day. But it was half an hour yet before his duties would recommence at the school. As he walked slowly along debating with himself how he should employ the time, a thought struck him; he hastened to the office of one of many agents for the locating and selling of Kentucky lands, and spent the interval in determining the titles to several tracts near town - an intricate matter in those times. But he found one farm, the part of an older military grant of the French and Indian wars, to which the title was unmistakably direct.

As soon as his school was out, he went to look at this property again, now that he was thinking of buying it. He knew it very well already, his walks having often brought him into its deep majestic woods; and he penetrated at once to an open knoll sloping toward the west and threw himself down on the deep green turf with the freedom of ownership.

VI

YES, this property would suit him; it would suit Amy. It was near town; it was not far from Major Falconer's. He could build his house on the hill-top where he was lying. At the foot of it, out of its limestone caverns, swelled a bountiful spring. As he listened he could hear the water of the branch that ran winding away from it toward the Elkhorn. That would be a pleasant sound when he sat with her in their doorway of summer evenings. On that southern slope he would plant his peach orchard, and he would have a vineyard. On this side Amy could have her garden, have her flowers. Sloping down from the front of the house to the branch would be their lawn, after he had cleared away everything but a few of the noblest old trees: under one of them, covered with a vine that fell in long green cascades from its summit to the ground, he would arrange a wild-grape swing for her, to make good the loss of the one she now had a" Major Falconer's.

Thus, out of one detail after another, he constructed the whole vision of the future, with the swiftness of desire, the unerring thoughtfulness of love; and, having transformed the wilderness into his home, he feasted on his banquet of ideas, his rich red wine of hopes and plans.

One of the subtlest, most saddening effects of the entire absence of possessions is the inevitable shrinkage of nature that must be undergone by those who have nothing to own. When a man, by some misfortune, has suddenly suffered the loss of his hands, much of the bewilderment and consternation that quickly follow have their origin in the thought that he never again shall be able to grasp. To his astonishment, he finds that no small part of his range of mental activity and sense of power was involved in that exercise alone. He has not lost merely his hands; much of his inner being has been stricken into disuse.

But the hand itself is only the rudest type of the universal necessity that pervades us to take hold. The body is furnished with two; the mind, the heart, the spirit - who shall number the invisible, the countless hands of these? All growth, all strength, all uplift, all power to rise in the world and to remain arisen, comes from the myriad hold we have taken upon higher surrounding realities.

Some time, wandering in a thinned wood, you may have happened upon an old vine, the seed of which had long ago been dropped and had sprouted in an open spot where there was no timber. Every May, in response to Nature's joyful bidding that it yet shall rise, the vine has loosed the thousand tendrils of its hope, those long, green, delicate fingers searching the empty air. Every December you may see these turned stiff and brown, and wound about themselves like spirals or knotted like the claw of a frozen bird. Year after year the vine has grown only at the head, remaining empty-handed; and the head itself, not being lifted always higher by anything the hands have seized, has but moved hither and thither, back and forth, like the head of a wounded snake in a path. Thus every summer you may see the vine, fallen back and coiled upon itself, and piled up before you like a low green mound, its own tomb; in winter a black heap, its own ruins. So, it often is with the poorest, who live on at the head, remaining empty-handed; fallen in and coiled back upon themselves, their own inescapable tombs, their own unavertible ruins. The prospect of having what to him was wealth had instantly bestowed upon John Gray the liberation of his strength. It had untied the hands of his idle powers; and the first thing he had reached fiercely out to grasp was Amy - his share in the possession of women; the second thing was land - his share in the possession of the earth. With these at the start, the one unshakable under his foot, the other inseparable from his side, he had no doubt that he should rise in the world and lay hold by steady degrees upon all that he should care to have. Naturally now these two blent far on and inseparably in the thoughts of one whose temperament doomed him always to be planning and striving for the future.

The last rays of the sun touched the summit of the knoll where he was lying. Its setting was with great majesty and repose, depth after depth of cloud opening inward as toward the presence of the infinite peace. The boughs of the trees overhead were in blossom; there were blue and white wild-flowers at his feet. As he looked about him, he said to himself in his solemn way that the long hard winter of his youth had ended; the springtime of his manhood was turning green like the woods.

With this night came his betrothal. For years he had looked forward to that as the highest white mountain peak of his life. As he drew near it now, his thoughts made a pathway for his feet, covering it as with a fresh fall of snow. Complete tenderness overcame him as he beheld Amy in this new sacred relation; a look of religious reverence for her filled his eyes. He asked himself what he had ever done to deserve all this. Perhaps it is the instinctive trait of most of us to seek an explanation for any great happiness as we are always prone to discuss the causes of our adversity. Accordingly, and in accord with our differing points of view of the universe, we declare of our joy that it is the gift of God to us despite our shortcomings and our transgressions; or that it is our blind share of things tossed out impersonally to us by the blind operation of the chances of life; or that it is the clearest strictest logic of our own being and doing - the natural vintage of our own grapes.

Of all these, the one that most deeply touches the heart is the faith, that a God above who alone knows and judges aright, still loves and has sent a blessing. To such a believer the heavens seem to have opened above his head, the Divine to have descended and returned; and left alone in the possession of his joy, he lifts his softened eyes to the Light, the Life, the Love, that has always guided him, always filled him, never forgotten him.

This stark audacity of faith was the schoolmaster's. It belonged to him through the Covenanter blood of his English forefathers and through his Scotch mother; but it had surrounded him also in the burning spiritual heroism of the time, when men wandered through the Western wilderness, girt as with camel's hair and fed as on locusts, but carrying from cabin to cabin, from post to post, through darkness and snow and storm the lonely banner of the Christ and preaching the gospel of everlasting peace to those who had never known any peace on earth. So that all his thoughts were linked with the eternal; he had threaded the labyrinth of life, evermore awestruck with its immensities and its mysteries; in his ear, he could plainly hear immortality sounding like a muffled bell across a sea, now near, now farther away, according as he was in danger or in safety. Therefore, his sudden prosperity - Amy - marriage - happiness - all these meant to him that Providence was blessing him.

In the depth of the wood it had grown dark. With all his thoughts of her sounding like the low notes of a cathedral organ, he rose and walked slowly back to town. He did not care for his supper; he did not wish to speak with any other person; the rude, coarse banter of the taverns and the streets would in some way throw a stain on her. Luckily he reached his room unaccosted; and then with care but without vanity having dressed himself in his best, he took his way to the house of Father Poythress.

VII

HE was kept waiting for some time. More than once he heard in the next room the sounds of smothered laughter and two voices, pitched in a confidential tone: the one with persistent appeal, the other with persistent refusal. At last there reached him the laughter of a merry agreement, and Amy entered the room, holding Kitty Poythress by the hand.

She had been looking all day for her lost bundle. Now she was tired; worried over the loss of her things which had been bought by her aunt at great cost and self-sacrifice; and disappointed that she should not be able to go to the ball on Thursday evening. It was to be the most brilliant assemblage of the aristocratic families of the town that had ever been known in the wilderness and the first endeavour to transplant beyond the mountains the old social elegance of Williamsburg, Annapolis, and Richmond. Not to be seen in the dress that Mrs. Falconer, dreaming of her own past, had deftly made - not to have her beauty reign absolute in that scene of lights and dance and music - it was the long, slow crucifixion of all the impulses of her gaiety and youth.

She did not wish to see any one to-night, least of all John Gray with whom she had had an engagement to go. No doubt he had come to ask why she had broken it in the note which she had sent him that morning. She had not given him any reason in the note; she did not intend to give him the reason now. He would merely look at her in his grave, reproachful, exasperating way and ask what was the difference: could she not wear some other dress? Or what great difference did it make whether she went at all? He was always ready to take this manner of patient forbearance toward her, as though she were one of his school children. To-night she was in no mood to have her troubles treated as trifles or herself soothed like an infant that was crying to be rocked.

She walked slowly into the room, dragging Kitty behind her. She let him press the tips of her unbending fingers, pouted, smiled faintly, dropped upon a divan by Kitty's side, strengthened her hold on Kitty's hand, and fixed her eyes on Kitty's hair. "Aren't you tired?" she said, giving it an absorbed caressing stroke, with a low laugh. "I am." "I am going to look again to-morrow, Kitty," she continued, brightening up with a decisive air, "and the next day and the next." She kept her face turned aside from John and did not include him in the conversation. Women who imagine themselves far finer ladies than this child was treat a man in this way - rarely - very rarely - say, once in the same man's lifetime.

"We are both so tired," she drowsily remarked at length, turning to John after some further parley which he did not understand and tapping her mouth prettily with the palm of her hand to fight away a yawn. "You know we've been riding all day. And William Penn is at death's door with hunger. Poor William Penn! I'm afraid he'll suffer to-night at the tavern stable. They never take care of him and feed him as I do at home.

He is so unhappy when be is hungry; and when he is unhappy, I am. And he has to be rubbed down so beautifully, or he doesn't shine." The tallow candles, which had been lighted when he came, needed snuffing by this time. The light was so dim that she could not see his face - blanched with bewilderment and pain and anger. What she did see as she looked across the room at him was his large black figure in an absent-minded awkward posture and his big head held very straight and high as though it were momentarily getting higher. He had remained simply silent. His silence irritated her; and she knew she was treating him badly and that irritated her with him all the more. She sent one of her light arrows at him barbed with further mischief.

"I wish, as you go back, you would stop at the stable and see whether they have mistreated him in any way. He takes things so hard when they don't go to suit him," and she turned to Kitty and laughed significantly.

Then she heard him clear his throat, and in a voice shaking with passion, he said:

"Give your orders to a servant." A moment of awkward silence followed. She did not recognize that voice as his or such rude, unreasonable words. "I suppose you want to know why I broke my engagement with you," she said, turning toward him aggrievedly and as though the subject could no longer be waived. "But I don't think you ought to ask for the reason. You ought to accept it without knowing it." "I do accept it. I had never meant to ask."

He spoke as though the whole affair were not worth recalling. She could not agree with him in this, and furthermore his manner administered a rebuke.

"Oh, don't be too indifferent," she said sarcastically, looking to Kitty for approval. If you cared to go to the party with me, you are supposed to be disappointed."

"I am disappointed," he replied briefly, but still with the tone of wishing to be done with the subject. Amy rose and snuffed the candles.

"And you really don't care to know why I broke my engagement?" she persisted, returning to her seat and seeing that she worried him.

"Not unless you should wish to tell me."

"But you should wish to know, whether I tell you or not. Suppose it were not a good reason?"

"I hadn't supposed you'd give me a poor one."

"At least, it's serious, Kitty."

"I had never doubted it."

"It might be amusing to you."

"It could hardly be both."

"Yes; it is both. It is serious and it is amusing."

He made no reply but by an impatient gesture.

"And you really don't wish to know?"He sat silent and still. "Then, I'll tell you: I lost the only reason I had for going," and she and Kitty exchanged a good deal of laughter of an innocent kind. The mood and the motive with which he had sought her made him feel that he was being unendurably trifled with and he rose. But at the same moment Kitty effected an escape and he and Amy were left alone. She looked quickly at the door through which Kitty had vanished, dropped her arms at her sides and uttered a little sigh of inexpressible relief.

"Sit down," she said, repeating her grimace at absent Kitty.

"You are not going! I want to talk to you. Isn't Kitty dreadful?"

Her voice and manner had changed. There was no one now before whom she could act - no one to whom she could show that she could slight him, play with him. Furthermore, she had gotten some relief from the tension of her ill humour by what she had already said; and now she really wanted to see him. The ill humour had not been very deep; nothing in her was very deep. And she was perfectly sincere again - for the moment. What does one expect?

"Don't look so solemn," she said with mock ruefulness. "You make me feel as though you had come to baptize me, as though you had to wash away my sins. Come here!" and she laid her hand invitingly on the chair that Kitty had vacated at her side.

He stood bolt upright in the middle of the room, looking down at her in silence. Then he walked slowly over and took the seat. She folded her hands over the back of her own chair, laid her cheek softly down on them and looked up with a smile - subdued, submissive, fond, absolutely his.

"Don't be cross!" she pleaded, with a low laugh full of maddening music to him.

He could not speak to her or look at her for anger and shame and disappointment; so she withdrew one hand from under her cheek and folded it softly over the back of his - his was pressed hard down on the cap of his knee - and took hold of his big finders one by one, caressing them.

"Don't be cross!" she pleaded. "Be good to me! I'm tired and unhappy!"

Still he would not speak, or look at her; so she put her hand back under her cheek again, and with a patient little sigh closed her eyes as though she had done all she could. The next moment she leaned over and let her forehead rest on the back of his hand."You are so cross!" she said. "I don't like you!"

"Amy!" he cried, turning fiercely on her and catching her hand cruelly in his, "before I say anything else to you, you've got to promise me - "And then he broke down and then went on again foolishly - ,you've got to promise me one thing now. You sha'n't treat me in one way when we are by ourselves and go in another way when other people are present. If you love me, as you always make me believe you do when we are alone, you must make the whole world believe it!"

"What right would I have to make the whole world believe I loved you?" she asked, looking at him quizzically.

"I'll give you the right!" The rattle of china at the cupboard in the next room was heard. Amy started up and skipped across the room to the candle on the mantelpiece.

"If Kitty does come back in here - " she said, in a disappointed undertone; and with the snuffers between her thumb and forefinger, she snipped them bitingly several times at the door. The door was opened slightly, a plate was thrust through, and a laughing voice called apologetically:

"Amy!"

"Come in here! Come in!" commanded Amy, delightedly; and as Kitty reluctantly entered, she fixed upon her a telling look. "Upon my word," she said, "what do you mean by treating me this way?" and catching Kitty's eye, she made a grimace at John.

Kitty offered the candy to John with the assurance that it was made out of that year's maple sugar in their own camp. "He never eats sweet things and he doesn't care for trifles: bring it here!" And the girls seated themselves busily side by side on the opposite side of the room. Amy bent over the plate and chose the largest, beautiful white plait."Now there'll be a long silence," she said, holding it up between her dainty fingers and settling herself back in her chair. "But, Kitty, you talk. And if you do leave your company again! - " She threatened Kitty charmingly.

He was in his room again, thinking it all over. She had not known why he had come: how could she know? To her it meant simply an ordinary call at an unfortunate hour; for she was tired - he could see that - and worried - he could see that also. And he! - had he ever been so solemn, so implacably in earnest, so impatient of the playfulness which at another time he would have found merely amusing? Why was he all at once growing so petty with her and exacting? Little by little he went over the circumstances judicially, in an effort to restore her to lovable supremacy over his imagination.

His imagination - for his heart was not in it. He wrought out her entire acquittal, but it did no good. Who at any time sounds the depths of the mind which, unlike the sea, can regain calm on the surface and remain troubled by a tempest at the bottom? What is the name of that imperial faculty dwelling within it which can annul the decisions of the other associated powers? After he had taken the entire blame upon himself, his rage and disappointment were greater than ever. Was it nothing for her to break her engagement with him and then to follow it up with treatment like that? Was it nothing to force Kitty into the parlour despite the silent understanding reached by all three long ago that whenever he called at the Poythress home, he would see her alone? Was it nothing to take advantage of his faithfulness to her, and treat him as though he had no spirit? Was it nothing to be shallow and silly herself?

Was it nothing - and ah! here was the trouble at the bottom of it all! Here was the strain of conviction pressing sorely, steadily in upon him through the tumult of his thoughts - was it nothing for her to be insincere? Did she even know what sincerity was? Would he marry an insincere woman? Insincerity was a growth not only ineradicable, but sure to spread over the nature as one grew older. He knew young people over whose minds it had begun to creep like the mere slip of a plant up a wall; old ones over whose minds it lay like a poisonous creeper hiding a rotting ruin. To be married and sit helplessly by and see this growth slowly sprouting outward from within, enveloping the woman he loved, concealing her, dragging her down - an unarrestable disease - was that to be his fate?

Was it already taking palpable possession of Amy? Could he hide his eyes any longer to the fact that he had felt its presence in her all the time - in its barely discoverable stages? What else could explain her conduct in allowing him, whenever they were alone, to think that she was fond of him, and then scattering this belief to the winds whenever others were present? Was this what Mrs. Falconer had meant? He could never feel any doubt of Mrs. Falconer. Merely to think of her now had the effect of instantly clearing the whole atmosphere for his baffled, bewildered mind.So the day ended. He had been beaten, routed, and by forces how insignificant! Bitterly he recalled his lesson to the children that morning. What a McGary he had been - reckless, overconfident, knowing neither theplan nor the resources of the enemy! He recalled his boast to Mrs. Falconer the day before, that he had never been defeated and that now he would proceed to carry out the plans of his life without interruption. But to-morrow evening, Amy would not be going to the ball. She would be alone. Then he would not go. He must find out all that he wished to know - or all that he did not.

VIII

THE evening of the ball had come at last. Not far from John's school on the square stood another log cabin, from which another and much more splendid light streamed out across the wilderness: this being the printing room and book-bindery of the great Mr. John Bradford. His portrait, scrutinized now from the distance and at the disadvantage of a hundred years, hands him down to posterity as a bald-headed man with a seedy growth of hair sprouting laterally from his temples, so that his ears look like little flat-boats half hidden in little canebrakes; with mutton-chop whiskers growing far up on the overhanging ledges of his cheek-bones and suggesting rather a daring variety of lichen; with a long arched nose, running on its own hook in a southwesterly direction; one eye a little higher than the other; a protruding upper lip, as though he had behind it a set of the false teeth of the time, which were fixed into the jaws by springs and hinges, all but compelling a man to keep his mouth shut by main force; and a very short neck with an overflowing jowl which weighed too heavily on his high shirt collar.

Despite his maligning portrait a foremost personage of his day, of indispensable substance, of invaluable port: Revolutionary soldier, Indian warrior; editor and proprietor of the Kentucky Gazette, the first newspaper in the wilderness; binder of its first books - some of his volumes still surviving on musty, forgotten shelves; senatorial elector; almanac-maker, taking his ideas from the greater Mr. Franklin of Philadelphia, as Mr. Franklin may have derived his from the still greater Mr. Jonathan Swift of London; appointed as chairman of the board of trustees to meet the first governor of the State when he had ridden into the town three years before and in behalf of the people of the new commonwealth which had been carried at last triumphantly into the Union, to bid his excellency welcome in an address conceived in the most sonorous English of the period; and afterwards for many years author of the now famous "Notes," which will perhaps make his name immortal among American historians. On this evening of the ball at the home of General James Wilkinson, the great Mr. Bradford was out of town, and that most unluckily; for the occasion - in addition to all the pleasure that it would furnish to the ladies - was designed as a means of calling together the leaders of the movement to separate Kentucky from the Union; and the idea may have been, that the great Mr. Bradford, having written one fine speech to celebrate her entrance, could as easily turn out a finer one to celebrate her withdrawal.

It must not be inferred that his absence had any political significance. He had merely gone a few days previous to the little settlement at Georgetown - named for the great George - to lay in a supply of paper for his Weekly, and had been detained there by heavy local rains, not risking so dry an article of merchandise either by pack-horse or open wagon under the dripping trees. Paper was very scarce in the wilderness and no man could afford to let a single piece get wet.

In setting out on his journey, he had instructed his sole

assistant - a young man by the name of Charles O'Bannon - as to his duties in the meantime: he was to cut some new capital letters out of a block of dog-wood in the office, and also some small letters where the type fell short; to collect if possible some unpaid subscriptions - this being one of the advantages that an editor always takes of his own absence - in particular to call upon certain merchants for arrears in advertisements; and he was to receive any lost articles that might be sent in to be advertised, or return such as should be called for by their owners: with other details appertaining to the establishment.

O'Bannon had performed his duties as he had been told - reserving for himself, as always, the right of a personal construction. He had addressed a written appeal to the nonpaying subscribers, declaring that the Gazette had now become a Try-Weekly, since Mr. Bradford had to try hard every week to get it out by the end; he had collected from several delinquent advertisers; whittled out three new capital letters, and also the face of Mr. Bradford and one of his legs; taken charge with especial interest of the department of Lost and Found and was now ready for other duties.

On this evening of the ball he was sitting in the office.

In one corner of the room stood a worn handpress with two dog-skin inking-balls. Between the logs of the wall near another corner a horizontal iron bar had been driven, and from the end of this bar hung a saucer-shaped iron lamp filled with bear-oil. Out of this oil stuck the end of a cotton rag for a wick; which, being set on fire, filled the room with a strong smell and a feeble, murky, flickering light. Under the lamp stood a plain oak slab on two pairs of crosslegs; and on the slab were papers and letters, a black ink-horn, some leaves of native tobacco, and a large gray-horn drinking-cup - empty. Under the table was a lately emptied bottle.O'Bannon sat in a rough chair before this drinking-cup, smoking a long tomahawk-pipe. His head was tilted backward, his eyes followed the flight of smoke upward.

That he expected to be at the party might have been inferred from his dress: a blue broadcloth coat with yellow gilt buttons; a swan's-down waistcoat with broad stripes of red and white; a pair of dove-coloured corded-velvet pantaloons with three large yellow buttons on the hips; and a neckcloth of fine white cambric.His figure was thickset, strong, cumbrous; his hair black, curly, shining. His eyes, bold, vivacious, and now inflamed, were of that rarely beautiful blue which is seen only in members of the Irish race. His complexion was a blending of the lily and the rose. His lips were thick and red under his short fuzzy moustache. His hands also were thick and soft, always warm, and not very clean - on account of the dog-skin inking-balls.

He had two ruling passions: the influence he thought himself entitled to exert over women; and his disposition to play practical jokes on men. Both the first and the second of these weaknesses grew out of his confidence that he had nothing to fear from either sex. Nevertheless he had felt forced to admit that his charms had never prevailed with Amy Falconer. He had often wondered how she could resist; but she had resisted without the least effort. Still, he pursued, and he had once told her with smiling candour that if she did not mind the pursuit, he did not mind the chase. Only, he never urged it into the presence of Mrs.

Falconer, of whom alone he stood in speechless, easily comprehensible awe. Perhaps to-night - as Amy had never seen him in ball-dress - she might begin to succumb; he had just placed her under obligation to him by an unexpected stroke of good fortune; and finally he had executed one neat stratagem at the expense of Mr. Bradford and another at the expense of John Gray. So that esteeming himself in a fair way to gratify one passion and having already gratified the other, he leaned back in his chair, smiling, smoking, drinking.

He had just risen to pinch the wick in the lamp overhead when a knock sounded on the door, and to his surprise and displeasure - for he thought he had bolted it - there entered without waiting to be bidden a low, broadchested, barefooted, blond fellow, his brown-tow breeches rolled up to his knees, showing a pair of fine white calves; a clean shirt thrown open at the neck and rolled up to the elbows, displaying a noble pair of arms; a ruddy shine on his good-humoured face; a drenched look about his short, thick, whitish hair; and a comfortable smell of soap emanating from his entire person.

Seeing him, O'Bannon looked less displeased; but keeping his seat and merely taking the pipe from his lips, he said, with an air of sarcasm, "I would have invited you to come in, Peter, but I see you have not waited for the invitation."

Peter deigned no reply; but walking forward, he clapped down on the oak slab a round handful of shillings and pence. "Count it, and see if it's all there," he said, taking a short cob pipe out of his mouth and planting his other hand stoutly on his hip. "What's this for?" O'Bannon spoke in a tone of wounded astonishment.

"What do you suppose it's for? Didn't I hear you've been out collecting?" "Well, you have had an advertisement running in the paper for some time." "That's what it's for then! And what's more, I've got the money to pay for a better one, whenever you'll write it."

"Sit down, sit down, sit down!" O'Bannon jumped from his chair, hurried across the room - a little unsteadily - emptied a pile of things on the floor, and dragged back a heavy oak stool. "Sit down. And Peter?" he added inquiringly, tapping his empty drinking-cup.

Peter nodded his willingness. O'Bannoli drew a key from his pocket and shook it temptingly under Peter's nose. Then he bolted the door and unlocked the cupboard, displaying a shelf filled with bottles.

"All for advertisements!" he said, waving his hand at the collection. "And a joke on Mr. Bradford. Fourth-proof French brandy, Jamaica rum, Holland gin, cherry bounce, Martinique cordial, Madeira, port, sherry, cider. All for advertisements! Two or three of these dealers have been running bills up, and to-day I stepped in and told them we'd submit to be paid in merchandise of this kind. And here's the merchandise. What brand of merchandise will you take?" "We had better take what you have been taking."

"As you please." He brought forward another drinking-cup and a bottle.

"Hold on!" cried Peter, laying a hand on his arm. "My

advertisement first!"

"As you please."

"About twice as long as the other one," instructed Peter. "As you please." O'Bannon set the bottle down, took up a goose-quill, and drew a sheet of paper before him.

"My business is increasing," prompted Peter still further, with a puzzled look as to what should come next. "Put that in!" "Of course," said O'Bannon. "I always put that in."

He was thinking impatiently about the ball and he wrote out something quickly and read it aloud with a thick, unsteady utterance:

"'Mr. Peter Springle continues to carry on the blacksmith business opposite the Sign of the Indian Queen. Mr. Springle cannot be rivalled in his shoeing of horses. He keeps on hand a constant supply of axes, chains, and hoes, which he will sell at prices usually asked - '"

"Stop," interrupted Peter who had sniffed a strange, delicious odour of personal praise in the second sentence. "You might say something more about me, before you bring in the axes."

"As you please."

"'Mr. Peter Springle executes his work with satisfaction and despatch; his work is second to none in Kentucky; no one surpasses him; he is a noted horseshoer; he does nothing but shoe horses.'" He looked at Peter inquiringly. "That sounds more like it," admitted Peter.

"Is that enough?"

"Oh, if that's all you can say!""'Mr. Springle devotes himself entirely to the shoeing of fine horses; fine horses are often injured by neglect in shoeing; Mr. Springle does not injure fine horses, but shoes them all around with new shoes at one dollar for each horse.'"

"Better," said Peter." Only, don't say so much about the horses! Say more about - "

"'Mr. Springle is the greatest blacksmith that ever left New Jersey - '""Or that ever lived I'll New Jersey."

O'Bannon rose and pinched the cotton wick, seized the bottle, and poured out more liquor.

"Peter," he said, squaring himself, "I'm going to let you into a secret. If you were not drunk, I wouldn't tell you. You'll forget it by morning."

"If I were half as drunk as you are, I couldn't listen," retorted Peter. "I don't want to know any secrets. I tell everything I know."

"You don't know any secrets? You don't know that last week Horatio Turpin sold a ten dollar horse in front of your shop for a hundred because he had - "

"Oh, I know some secrets about horses," admitted Peter, carelessly. "It's a secret about a horse I'm going to tell you," said O'Bannon.

"Here is an advertisement that has been left to be

inserted in the next paper: 'Lost, on Tuesday evening, on the road between Frankfort and Lexington, a bundle of clothes tied up in a blue-and-white checked cotton neckerchief, and containing one white muslin dress, a pale-blue silk coat, two thin white muslin handkerchiefs, one pair long kid gloves - straw colour - one pair white kid shoes, two cambric handkerchiefs, and some other things. Whoever will deliver said clothes to the printer, or give information so that they can be got, will be liberally rewarded on application to him.'

"And here, Peter, is another advertisement. Found, on Tuesday evening, on the road between Lexington and Frankfort, a bundle of clothes tied in a blue-and-white neckerchief. The owner can recover property by calling on the printer.'"

He pushed the papers away from him.

"Yesterday morning who should slip around here but Amy Falconer. And then, in such a voice, she began. How she had come to town the day before, and had brought her party dress. How the bundle was lost. How she had come to inquire whether any one had left the clothes to be advertised; or whether I wouldn't put an advertisement in the paper; or, if they were left at my office before Thursday evening, whether I wouldn't send them to her at once."

"Ahem!" said Peter drily, but with moisture in his eyes.

"She hadn't more than gone before who should come in here but a boy bringing this same bundle of clothes with a note from John Gray, saying that he had found them in the public road yesterday, and asking me to send them at once to the owner, if I should hear who

James Lane Allen

she was; if not, to advertise them."

"That's no secret," said Peter contemptuously.

"I might have sent that bundle straight to the owner of it. But, when I have anything against a man, I always forgive him, only I get even with him first."

"What are you hammering at?" cried Peter, bringing his fist down on the table. "Hit the nail on the head."

"Now I've got no grudge against her," continued O'Bannon. "I'd hate her if I could. I've tried hard enough, but I can't. She may treat me as she pleases: it's all the same to me as soon as she smiles. But as for this redheaded Scotch-Irishman - "

"Stop!" said Peter. "Not a word against him!" O'Bannon stared.

"He's no friend of yours," said he, reflectively.

"He is!"

"Oh, is he? Well, only the other day I heard him say that he thought a good deal more of your shoes than he did of you," cried O'Bannon, laughing sarcastically.

Peter made no reply, but his neck seemed to swell and his face to be getting purple.

"And he's a friend of yours? I can't even play a little joke on him." "Play your joke on him!" exclaimed Peter, "and when my time comes, I'll play mine." "When he sent the bundle here yesterday morning I could have returned it straight to her. I locked it in that closet! 'You'll never go to the ball with her,' I said, 'if I have to keep her away.' I set my trap. To-day I hunted up Joseph Holden. 'Come by the office, as you are on your way to the party to-night,' I said. 'I want to talk to you about a piece of land. Come early; then we can go together.' When he came - just before you did - I said, 'Look here, did you know that Amy wouldn't be at the ball? She lost her clothes as she was coming to town the other day, and somebody has just sent them here to be advertised. I think I'd better take them around to her yet: it's not too late.' 'I'll take them! I'll go with her myself!' he cried, jumping up.

"So she'll be there, he'll be there, I'll be there, we'll all be there - but your John can hear about it in the morning." And O'Bannon arose slowly, but unexpectedly sat down again.

"You think I won't be there," he said threateningly to Peter. "You think I'm drunk. I'll show you! I'll show you that I can walk - that I can dance - dance by myself - do it all - by myself - furnish the music and do the dancing."

He began whistling "Sir Roger de Coverley," and stood up, but sank down again and reached for the bottle.

"Peter," he said with a soft smile, looking down at his gorgeous swan's-down waistcoat and his well-shaped dove-coloured legs: "ain't I a beauty?" "Yes, you are a beauty!" said Peter.

Suddenly lifting one of his bare feet, he shot O'Bannon as by the action of a catapult against the printing-press.

He lay there all night.

IX

HOW fine a thing it would be if all the faculties of the mind could be trained for the battles of life as a modern nation makes every man a soldier. Some of these, as we know, are always engaged in active service; but there are times when they need to be strengthened by others, constituting a first reserve; and yet graver emergencies arise in the marchings of every man when the last defences of land and hearth should be ready to turn out: too often even then the entire disciplined strength of his forces would count as a mere handful to the great allied powers of the world and the devil.

But so few of our faculties are of a truly military turn, and these wax indolent and unwary from disuse like troops during long times of peace. We all come to recognize sooner or later, of course, the unfailing little band of them that form our standby, our battle-smoked campaigners, our Old Guard, that dies, never-surrenders. Who of us also but knows his faithful artillery, dragging along his big guns - and so liable to reach the scene after the fighting is over? Who when worsted has not fought many a battle through again merely to show how different the result would have been, if his artillery had only arrived in time! Boom! boom! boom! Where are the enemy now? And who does not take pride in his navy, sweeping the high seas of the imagination but too often departed for some foreign port when the coast defences need protecting?

Beyond this general dismemberment of our resources do we not all feel the presence within us of certain renegades? Does there not exist inside every man a certain big, ferocious-looking faculty who is his drum major - loving to strut at the head of a peaceful parade and twirl his bawble and roll his eyes at the children and scowl back at the quiet intrepid fellows behind as though they were his personal prisoners? Let but a skirmish threaten, and our dear, ferocious, fat major - ! not even in the rear - not even on the field! Then there is a rattling little mannikin who sleeps in the barracks of the brain and is good for nothing but to beat the cerebral drum. There is a certain awkward squad - too easily identified - who have been drafted again and again into service only to be in the way of every skilled manoeuvre, only to be mustered out as raw recruits at the very end of life. And, finally, there is a miscell-aneous crowd of our faculties scattered far and near at their humdrum peaceful occupations; so that if a quick call for war be heard, these do but behave as a populace that rushes into a street to gaze at the national guard already marching past, some of the spectators not even grateful, not even cheering.

All that day John had to fight a battle for which he had never been trained; moreover he had been compelled to divide his forces: there was the far-off solemn battle going on in his private thoughts; and there was the usual siege of duties in the school. For once he would gladly have shirked the latter; but the single compensation he always tried to wrest from the disagreeable things of life was to do them in such a way that they would never fester in his conscience like

James Lane Allen

thorns broken off in the flesh.

During the forenoon, therefore, by an effort which only those who have experienced it can understand, he ordered off all communication with larger troubles and confined himself in that stifling prison-house of the mind where the perplexities and toils of childhood become enormous and everything else in the world grows small. Up under the joists there was the terrible struggle of a fly in a web, at first more and more violent, then ceasing in a strain so fine that the ear could scarce take it; a bee came in one window, went out another; a rat, sniffing greedily at its hole, crept toward a crumb under a bench, ran back, crept nearer, seized it and was gone; a toiling slate-pencil grated on its way as arduously as a wagon up a hill; he had to teach a beginner its letters. These were the great happenings. At noon the same child that had brought him a note on the day before came with another:

"Kitty is going to the ball with Horatio. I shall be alone. We can have our talk uninterrupted. How unreasonable you are! Why don't you understand things without wanting to have them explained? If you wish to go to the ball, you can do this afterwards. Don't come till Kitty has gone."

Duties in the school till near sunset, then letters. O'Bannon had told him that Mr. Bradford's post-rider would leave at four o'clock next morning; if he had letters to send, they must be deposited in the box that night. Gray had letters of the utmost importance to write - to his lawyer regarding the late decision in his will case, and to the secretary of the Democratic Club in Philadelphia touching the revival of activity in the clubs throughout the country on account of the expected treaty with England.

After he had finished them, he strolled slowly about the dark town - past his school-house, thinking that his teaching days would soon be over - past Peter's blacksmith shop, thinking what a good fellow he always was - past Mr. Bradford's editorial room, with a light under the door and the curtain drawn across the window. Two or three times he lingered before show-windows of merchandise. He had some taste in snuff-boxes, being the inheritor of several from his Scotch and Irish ancestors, and there were a few in the new silversmith's window which he found little to his liking. As he passed a tavern, a group of Revolutionary officers, not yet gone to the ball, were having a time of it over their pipes and memories; and he paused to hear one finish a yarn of strong fibre about the battle of King's Mountain. Couples went hurrying by him beautifully dressed. Once down a dark street he fancied that he distinguished Amy's laughter ringing faintly out on the still air; and once down another he clearly heard the long cry of a pet panther kept by a young backwoods hunter.

The Poythress homestead was wrapped in silence as he stepped upon the porch; but the door was open, there was a light inside, and by means of this he discovered, lying asleep on the threshold, a lad who was apprentice to the new English silversmith of the town and a lodger at the minister's - the bond of acquaintanceship being the memory of John Wesley who had sprinkled the lad's father in England.

John laid a hand on his shoulder and tried to break his slumber. He opened his eyes at last and said, "Nobody at home," and went to sleep again. When thoroughly aroused, he sat up. Mr. and Mrs. Poythress had been called away to some sick person; they had asked him to sit up till they came back; he wished they'd come; he didn't see how he was ever to learn how to make watches if he couldn't get any sleep; and be lay down again.

John aroused him again.

"Miss Falconer is here; will you tell her I wish to see her?"

The lad didn't open his eyes but said dreamily:

"She's not here; she's gone to the party."

John lifted him and set him on his feet. Then he put his hands on his shoulders and shook him:

"You are asleep! Wake up! Tell Miss Falconer I wish to see her." The lad seized Gray by the arms and shook him with all his might.

"You wake up," he cried. "I tell you she's gone to the party. Do you hear? She's gone to the party! Now go away, will you? How am I ever to be a silversmith, if I can't get any sleep?" And stretching himself once more on the settee, he closed his eyes.

John turned straight to the Wilkinsons'. His gait was not hurried; whatever his face may have expressed was hidden by the darkness. The tense quietude of his mind was like that of a summer tree, not one of whose thousands of leaves quivers along the edge, but toward which a tempest is rolling in the distance.

The house was set close to the street. The windows were open; long bars of light fell out; as he stepped forward to the threshold, the fiddlers struck up "Sir Roger de Coverley"; the company parted in lines to the right and left, leaving a vacant space down the middle of the room; and into this vacant space he saw Joseph lead Amy and the two begin to dance. She wore a white muslin dress - a little skillful work had restored its freshness; a blue silk coat of the loveliest hue; a wide white lace tucker caught across her round bosom with a bunch of cinnamon roses; and straw-coloured kid gloves, reaching far up her snow-white arms. Her hair was coiled high on the crown of her head and airily overtopped by a great curiously carved silver-and-tortoise-shell comb; and under her dress played the white mice of her feet. The tints of her skin were pearl and rose; her red lips parted in smiles. She was radiant with excitement, happiness, youth. She culled admiration, visiting all eyes with hers as a bee all flowers. It was not the flowers she cared for.

He did not see her dress; he did not recognize the garments that had hung on the wall of his room. What he did see and continued to see was the fact that she was there and dancing with Joseph.

If he had stepped on a rattlesnake, he could not have been more horribly, more miserably stung. He had the sense of being poisoned, as though actual venom were coursing through his blood. There was one swift backward movement of his mind over the chain of forerunning events.

"She is a venomous little serpent!" he groaned aloud. "And I have been crawling in the dust to her, to be stung like this!" He walked quietly into the house.

He sought his hostess first. He found her in the centre of a group of ladies, wearing the toilet of the past Revolutionary period in the capitals of the East. The vision dazzled him, bewildered him. But he swept his eye over them with one feeling of heart-sickness and asked his hostess one question: was Mrs. Falconer there? She was not.

In another room he found his host, and a group of Revolutionary officers and other tried historic men, surrounding the Governor. They were discussing the letters that had passed between the President and his Excellency for the suppression of a revolution in Kentucky. During this spring of 1795 the news had reached Kentucky that Jay had at last concluded a treaty with England. The ratification of this was to be followed by the surrender of those terrible North-western posts that for twenty years had been the source of destruction and despair to the single-handed, maddened, or massacred Kentuckians. Behind those forts had rested the inexhaustible power of the Indian confederacies, of Canada, of England. Out of them, summer after summer, armies that knew no pity had swarmed down upon the doggedly advancing line of the Anglo-Saxon frontiersmen. Against them, some-times unaided, sometimes with the aid of Virginia or of the National Government, the pioneers hurled their frantic retaliating armies: Clarke and Boone and Kenton often and often; Harmar followed by St. Clair; St. Clair followed by Wayne. It was for the old failure to give aid against these that Kentucky had hated Virginia and resolved to tear herself loose from the mother State and either perish or triumph alone. It was for the failure to give aid against these that Kentucky hated Washington, hated the East, hated the National Government, and plotted to wrest Kentucky away from the Union, and either make her an independent power or ally her with France or Spain.

But over the sea now France - France that had come to the rescue of the colonies in their struggle for independence - this same beautiful, passionate France was fighting all Europe unaided and victorious. The spectacle had amazed the world. In no other spot had sympathy been more fiercely kindled than along that Western border where life was always tense with martial passion. It had passed from station to station, like a torch blazing in the darkness and with a two-forked fire - gratitude to France, hatred of England - hatred rankling in a people who had come out of the very heart of the English stock as you would hew the heart out of a tree. So that when, two years before this, Citizen Genet, the ambassador of the French republic, had landed at Charleston, been driven through the country to New York amid the acclamations of French sympathizers, and disregarding the President'sproclamation of neutrality, had begun to equip privateers and enlist crews to act against the commerce of England and Spain, it was to the backwoodsmen of Kentucky that he sent four agents, to enlist an army, appoint a generalissimo, and descend upon the Spanish settlements at the mouth of the Mississippi - those same hated settlements that had refused to the Kentuckians the right of navigation for their commerce, thus shutting them off from the world by water, as the mountains shut them off from the world by land.

Hence the Jacobin clubs that were formed in Kentucky: one at Lexington, a second at Georgetown, a third at Paris. Hence the liberty poles in the streets of the towns; the tricoloured cockades on the hats of the men; the hot blood between the anti-federal and the federalist parties of the State.

The actions of Citizen Genet had indeed been disavowed by his republic. But the sympathy for France, the hatred of England and of Spain, had but grown meantime; and when therefore in this spring of 1795 the news reached the frontier that Jay had concluded a treaty with England - the very treaty that would bring to the Kentuckians the end of all their troubles with the posts of the Northwest - the flame of revolution blazed out with greater brilliancy.

During the hour that John Gray spent in that assemblage of men that night, the talk led always to the same front of offence: the baser truckling to England, an old enemy; the baser desertion of France, a friend. He listened to one man of commanding eloquence, while he traced the treaty to the attachment of Washington for aristocratic institutions; to another who referred it to the jealousy felt by the Eastern congressmen regarding the growth of the new power beyond the Alleghanies; to a third who foretold that like all foregoing pledges it would leave Kentucky still exposed to the fury of the Northern Indians; to a fourth who declared that let the treaty be once ratified with Lord Granville, and in the same old faithless way, nothing more would be done to extort from Spain for Kentucky the open passage of the Mississippi.

At any other time he would have borne his part in these discussions. Now he scarcely heard them. All the forces of his mind were away, on another battle-field and he longed to be absent with them, a field strewn with the sorrowful carnage of ideal and hope and plan, home, happiness, love. He was hardly aware that his own actions must seem unusual, until one of the older men took him affectionately by the hand and said:

"Marshall tells me that you teach school till sunset and read law till sunrise; and tonight you come here with your eyes blazing and your skin as pallid and dry as a monk's. Take off the leeches of the law for a good month, John! They abstract too much blood. If the Senate ratifies in June the treachery of Jay and Lord Granville, there will be more work than ever for the Democratic Societies in this country, and nowhere more than in Kentucky. We shall need you then more than the law needs you now, or than you need it. Save yourself for the cause of your tricolour. You shall have a chance to rub the velvet off your antlers."

"We shall soon put him beyond the reach of his law," said a member of the Transylvania Library Committee. "As soon as his school is out, we are going to send him to ask subscriptions from the President, the Vice-President, and others, and then on to Philadelphia to buy the books."

A shadow fell upon the face of another officer, and in a lowered tone he said, with cold emphasis: "I am sorry that the citizens of this town should stoop to ask anything from such a man as George Washington."

The schoolmaster scarcely realized what he had done when he consented to act as a secret emissary of the Jacobin Club of Lexington to the club in Philadelphia during the summer.

The political talk ended at last, the gentlemen returned to the ladies. He found himself standing in a doorway beside an elderly man of the most polished hearing and graceful manners, who was watching a minuet.

"Ah!" he said, waving his hand with delight toward the scene. "This is Virginia and Maryland brought into the West! It reminds me of the days when I danced with Martha Custis and Dolly Madison. Some day, with a beginning like this, Kentucky will be celebrated for its beautiful women. The daughters and the grand-daughters and the great-granddaughters of such mothers as these - "

"And of fathers like these!" interposed one of the town trustees who came up at that moment. "But for the sake of these ladies isn't it time we were passing a law against the keeping of pet panthers? I heard the cry of one as I came here to-night. What can we do with these young backwoods hunters? Will civilization ever make pets of them - ever tame them?" John felt some one touch his arm; it was Kitty with Horatio. Her cheeks were like poppies; her good kind eyes welcomed him sincerely.

"You here! I'm so glad. Haven't you seen Amy? She is in the other room with Joseph. Have they explained everything? But we will loose our place - "she cried, and with a sweet smile of adieu to him, and of warning to her partner, she glided away.

"We are entered for this horse race," remarked Mr. Turpin, lingering a moment longer. "Weight for age, agreeable to the rules of New Market. Each subscriber to pay one guinea, etc., etc., etc." He was known as the rising young turfman of the town, having first run his horses down Water Street; but future member of the first Jockey Club; so that in the full blossom of his power he could name all the horses of his day with the pedigree of each: beginning with Tiger by Tiger, and on through Sea Serpent by Shylock, and Diamond by

Brilliant, and Black Snake by Sky Lark: a type of man whom long association with the refined and noble nature of the horse only vulgarizes and disennobles.

Once afterward Gray's glance fell on Amy and Joseph across the room. They were looking at him and laughing at his expense and the sight burnt his eyes as though hot needles had been run into them. They beckoned gaily, but he gave no sign; and in a moment they were lost behind the shifting figures of the company. While he was dancing, however, Joseph came up.

"As soon as you get away, Amy wants to see you."

Half and hour later he came a second time and drew Gray aside from a group of gentlemen, speaking more seriously: "Amy wants to explain how all this happened. Come at once."

"There is nothing to explain," said John, with indifference. Joseph answered reproachfully: "This is foolish, John! When you know what has passed, you will not censure her. And I could not have done otherwise." Despite his wish to be serious, he could not help laughing for he was very happy himself.

But to John Gray these reasonable words went for the very thing that they did not mean. His mind had been forced to a false point of view; and from a false point of view the truth itself always looks false. Moreover it was intolerable that Joseph should be defending to him the very woman whom a few hours before he had hoped to marry. "There is no explanation needed from her," he replied, with the same indifference. "I think I understand. What I do not understand I should rather take for granted. But you, Joseph, you owe me an explanation. This is not the place to give it." His face twitched, and he knotted the fingers of his large hands together like bands of iron. "But by God I'll have it; and if it is not a good one, you shall answer." His oath sounded like an invocation to the Divine justice - not profanity. Joseph fixed his quiet fearless eyes on Gray's. "I'll answer for myself - and for her" - he replied and turned away.

Still later Gray met her while dancing - the faint rose of her cheeks a shade deeper, the dazzling whiteness of her skin more pearl-like with warmth, her gaiety and happiness still mounting, her eyes still wandering among the men, culling their admiration.

"You haven't asked me to dance to-night. You haven't even let me tell you why I had to come with Joseph, when I wanted to come with you." She gave a little pout of annoyance and let her eyes rest on his with the old fondness. "Don't you want to know why I broke my engagement with you?" And she danced on, smiling back at him provokingly. He did not show that he heard; and although they did not meet again, he was made aware that a change had at last come over her. She was angry now. He could hear her laughter oftener - laughter that was meant for his ear and she was dancing oftener with Joseph. He looked at her repeatedly, but she avoided his eyes.

"I am playing a poor part by staying here!" he said with shame, and left the house.

After wandering aimlessly about the town for some two hours, he went resolvedly back again and stood out in the darkness, looking in at her through the windows. There she was, unwearied, happy, not feigning; and no more affected by what had taken place between them than a candle is affected by a scorched insect. So it seemed to him.

This was the first time he had ever seen her at a ball. He had never realized what powers she possessed in a field like this: what play, what resources, what changes, what stratagems, what victories. He mournfully missed for the first time certain things in himself that should have corresponded with all those light and graceful things in her. Perhaps what hurt him most were her eyes, always abroad searching for admiration, forever filling the forever emptied honeycomb of self-love.

With him love was a sacred, a grim, an inviolate selection. He would no more have wished the woman he had chosen to seek indiscriminate admiration with her eyes than with her lips or her waist. It implied the same fatal flaw in her refinement, her modesty, her faithfulness, her high breeding. A light wind stirred the leaves of the trees overhead. A few drops of rain fell on his hat. He drew his hand heavily across his eyes and turned away. Reaching his room, he dropped down into a chair before his open window and sat gazing absently into the black east.

Within he faced a yet blacker void - the ruined hopes on which the sun would never rise again.

It was the end of everything between him and Amy: that was his one thought. It did not occur to him even to reflect whether he had been right or wrong, rude or gentle: it was the end: nothing else appeared worth considering.

James Lane Allen

Life to him meant a simple straightforward game played with a few well-known principles. It must be as open as a chess-board: each player should see every move of the other: and all who chose could look on.

He was still very young.

X

THE glimmer of gray dawn at last and he had never moved from his seat. A fine, drizzling rain had set in. Clouds of mist brushed against the walls of his cabin. In the stillness he could hear the big trees shedding their drops from leaf to bending leaf and the musical tinkle of these as they took their last leap into little pools below. With the chilliness which misery brings he got up at last and wrapped his weather-coat about him. If it were only day when he could go to his work and try to forget! Restless, sleepless, unable to read, tired of sitting, driven on by the desire to get rid of his own thoughts, he started out to walk. As he passed his school-house he noticed that the door of it, always fastened by a simple latch, now stood open; and he went over to see if everything inside were in order. All his life, when any trouble had come upon him, he had quickly returned to his nearest post of duty like a soldier; and once in the school-room now, he threw himself down in his chair with the sudden feeling that here in his familiar work he must still find his home - the home of his mind and his affections - as so long in the past. The mere aspect of the poor bare place had never been so kind. The very walls appeared to open to him like a refuge, to enfold themselves around him with friendly strength and understanding.

He sat at the upper end of the room, gazing blankly

James Lane Allen

through the doorway at the gray light and clouds of white mist trailing. Once an object came into the field of his vision. At the first glimpse he thought it a dog - long, lean, skulking, prowling, tawny - on the scent of his tracks. Then the mist passed over it. When he beheld it again it had approached nearer and was creeping rapidly toward the door. His listless eyes grew fascinated by its motions - its litheness, suppleness, grace, stealth, exquisite caution. Never before had he seen a dog with the step of a cat. A second time the fog closed over it, and then, advancing right out of the cloud with more swiftness, more cunning, its large feet falling as lightly as flakes of snow, the weight of its huge body borne forward as noiselessly as the trailing mist, it came straight on. It reached the hickory block, which formed the doorstep; it paused there an instant, with its fore quarters in the doorway, one fore foot raised, the end of its long tail waving; and then it stole just over the threshold and crouched, its head pressed down until its long, whitish throat lay on the floor; its short, jagged ears set forward stiffly like the broken points of a javelin; its dilated eye blazing with steady green fire - as still as death. And then with his blood become as ice in his veins from horror and all the strength gone out of him in a deathlike faintness, the school- master realized that he was face to face unarmed with a cougar, gaunt with famine and come for its kill.

This dreaded animal, the panther or painter of the backwoodsman, which has for its kindred the royal tiger and the fatal leopard of the Old World, the beautiful ocelot and splendid unconquerable jaguar of the New, is now rarely found in the Atlantic States or the fastnesses of the Alleghanies. It too has crossed the Mississippi and is probably now best known as the savage puma of more southern zones. But a hundred years ago it abounded throughout the Western wilderness, making its deeper dens in the caverns of mountain rocks, its lair in the impenetrable thickets of bramble and brakes of cane, or close to miry swamps and watery everglades; and no other region was so loved by it as the vast game park of the Indians, where reined a semi-tropical splendour and luxuriance of vegetation and where, protected from time immemorial by the Indian hunters themselves, all the other animals thatconstitute its prey roved and ranged in unimaginable numbers. To the earliest Kentuckians who cut their way into this, the most royal jungle of the New World, to wrest it from the Indians and subdue it for wife and child, it was the noiseless nocturnal cougar that filled their imaginations with the last degree of dread. To them its cry - most peculiar and startling at the love season, at other times described as like the wail of a child or of a traveller lost in the woods - aroused more terror than the nearest bark of the wolf; its stealth and cunning more than the strength and courage and address of the bear; its attack more than the rush of the majestic, resistless bison, or the furious pass with antlers lowered of the noble, ambereyed, infuriated elk. Hidden as still as an adder in long grass of its own hue, or squat on a log, or amid the foliage of a sloping tree, it waited around the salt licks and the springs and along the woodland pathways for the other wild creatures. It possessed the strength to kill and drag a heifer to its lair; it would leap upon the horse of a traveller and hang there unshaken, while with fang and claw it lacerated the hind quarters and the flanks - as the tiger of India tries to hamstring its nobler, unmanageable victims; or let an unwary bullock but sink a little way in a swamp and it was upon him, rending him, devouring him, in his long agony.

Some hunter once had encamped at the foot of a tree, cooked his supper, seen his fire die out and lain down to sleep, with only the infinite solitude of the woods for his blanket, with the dreary, dismal silence for his pillow. Opening his eyes to look up for the last time at the peaceful stars, what he perceived above him were two nearer stars set close together, burning with a green light, never twinkling. Or another was startled out of sleep by the terrible cry of his tethered horse. Or after a long, ominous growl, the cougar had sprung against his tent, knocking it away as a squirrel would knock the thin shell from a nut to reach the kernel; or at the edge of the thicket of tall grass he had struck his foot against the skeleton of some unknown hunter, dragged down long before.

To such adventures with all their natural exaggeration John Gray had listened many a time as they were recited by old hunters regarding earlier days in the wilderness; for at this period it was thought that the cougar had retreated even from the few cane-brakes that remained unexplored near the settlements. But the deer, timidest of animals, with fatal persistence returns again and again to its old-time ranges and coverts long after the bison, the bear, and the elk have wisely abandoned theirs; and the cougar besets the deer.

It was these stories that he remembered now and that filled him with horror, with the faintness of death. His turn had come at last, he said; and as to the others, it had come without warning. He was too shackled with weakness to cry out, to stand up. The windows on each side were fastened; there was no escape. There was nothing in the room on which he could lay hold - no weapon or piece of wood, or bar of iron. If a struggle took place, it would be a clean contest between will and will, courage and courage, strength and strength, the love of prey and the love of life.It was well for him that this was not the first time he had ever faced death, as he had supposed; and that the first thought that had rushed into his consciousness before returned to him now. That thought was this: that death had come far too soon, putting an end to his plans to live, to act, to succeed, to make a great and a good place for himself in this world before he should leave it for another. Out of this a second idea now liberated itself with incredible quickness and spread through him like a living flame: it was his lifelong attitude of victory, his lifelong determination that no matter what opposed him he must conquer. Young as he was, this triumphant habit had already yielded him its due result that growth of character which arises silently within us, built up out of a myriad nameless elements - beginning at the very bottom of the ocean of unconsciousness; growing as from cell to cell, atom to atom - the mere dust of victorious experience - the hardening deposits of the ever-living, ever-working, ever-rising will; until at last, based on eternal quietude below and lifting its wreath of palms above the waves of life, it stands finished, indestructible, our inward rock of defence against every earthly storm.

Soon his face was worth going far to see. He had grown perfectly calm. His weakness had been followed by a sense of strength wholly extraordinary. His old training in the rough athletics of the wilderness had made him supple, agile, wary, long-winded. His eyes hadnever known what it was to be subdued; he had never taken them from the cougar.

Keeping them on it still, he rose slowly from the chair, realizing that his chances would be better if he were in the middle of the room. He stepped round in front of his table and walked two paces straight forward and then paused, his face as white, as terrible, as death. At the instant of his moving he could see the tense drawing in of all the muscles of the cougar and the ripple of its skin, as its whole body quivered with excitement and desire; and he knew that as soon as he stopped it would make its spring.

With a growl that announces that all hiding and stealth are over, the leap came. He had thrown his body slightly forward to meet it with the last thought that whatever happened he must guard his throat. It was at this that the cougar aimed, leaping almost perpendicularly, its widespread fore feet reaching for his shoulders, while the hind feet grasped at his legs. The under part of its body being thus exposed, he dealt it a blow with all his strength - full in the belly with his foot, and hurled it backward. For a second it crouched again, measuring him anew, then sprang again. Again he struck, but this time the fore feet caught his arm as they passed backward; the sharp, retractile nails tore their way across the back and palm of his hand like dull knives and the blood gushed. Instantly the cougar leaped upon the long, wooden desk that ran alone one side of the room, and from that advantage, sprang again but he bent his body low so that it passed clean over him. Instantly it was upon his desk at his back; and before he could more than recover his balance and turn, it sprang for the fourth time. He threw out his arm to save his throat, but the cougar had reached his left shoulder, struck its claws deep into his heavy coat; and with a deafening roar sounding close in his ears, had buried its fangs near the base of his neck, until he heard them click as they met through his flesh.

He staggered, but the desk behind caught him. Straightening himself up, and grappling the panther with all his strength as he would a man, he turned with it and bent it over the sharp edge of the ponderous desk, lower, lower, trying to break its back. One of the fore feet was beginning to tear through his clothing, and straightening himself up again, he reached down and caught this foot and tried to bend it, break it. He threw himself with all his force upon the floor, falling with the cougar under him, trying to crush it. He staggered to his feet again, but stepped on his own blood and fell. And then, feeling his blood trickling down his breast and his strength going, with one last effort he put up his hands and seizing the throat, fastened his fingers like iron rivets around the windpipe. And then - with the long, loud, hoarse, despairing roar with which a man, his mouth half full of water, sinks far out in the ocean - he fell again.

XI

IT was ten o'clock that morning of mid-May. The rain was over. Clouds and mists were gone, leaving an atmosphere of purest crystal. The sun floated a globe of gold in the yielding blue. Above the wilderness on a dead treetop, the perch of an eagle now flashing like a yellow weather-vane, a thrush poured the spray-like far-falling fountain of his notes over upon the bowed woods. Beneath him the dull green domes of the trees flashed as though inlaid with gems, white and rose. Under these domes the wild grapevines, climbing the forest arches as the oak of stone climbs the arches of a cathedral, filled the ceiling and all the shadowy spaces between with fresh outbursts of their voluptuous dew-born fragrance. And around the rough-haired Satyr feet of these vines the wild hyacinth, too full of its own honey to stand, fell back on its couch of moss waiting to be visited by the singing bee.

The whole woods emerged from the cloudy bath of Nature with the coolness, the freshness, the immortal purity of Diana united to the roseate glow and mortal tenderness of Venus; and haunted by two spirits: the chaste, unfading youth of Endymion and the dust-born warmth and eagerness of Dionysus.

Through these woods, feeling neither their heat nor their cold, secured by Nature against any passion for either the cooling star or the inflaming dust, rode Amy - slowly homeward from the ball. Yet lovelier, happier than anything the forest held. She had pushed her bonnet entirely off so that it hung by the strings at the back of her neck; and her face emerged from the round sheath of it like a pink and white tulip, newly risen and bursting forth.

When she reached home, she turned the old horse loose with many pattings and good-byes and promises of maple sugar later in the day; and then she bounded away to the garden to her aunt, of whom, perhaps, she was more truly fond than of any one in the world except herself.

Mrs. Falconer had quickly left off work and was advancing very slowly - with mingled haste and reluctance - to meet her. "Aunt Jessica! Aunt Jessica!" cried Amy in a voice that rang like a small silver bell, "I haven't seen you for two whole nights and three whole days!" Placing her hands on Mrs. Falconer's shoulders, she kissed her once on each cheek and twice playfully on the pearly tip of the chin; and then she looked into her eyes as innocently as a perfect tulip might look at a perfect rose.

Mrs. Falconer smilingly leaned forward and touched her lips to Amy's forehead. The caress was as light as thistle-down - perhaps no warmer.

"Three entire days!" she said chidingly. "It has been three months," and she searched through Amy's eyes onward along the tortuous little passages of her heart as a calm blue air might search the chambers of a cold beautiful sea-shell.

Each of these women instantly perceived that since they had parted a change had taken place in the other; neither was aware that the other noticed the change in herself. Mrs. Falconer had been dreading to find one in Amy when she should come home; and it was the one she saw now that fell as a chill upon her. Amy was triumphantly aware of a decisive change in herself, but chose for the present, as she thought, to keep it hidden; and as for any change in her aunt - that was an affair of less importance.

"Why, Aunt Jessica!" she exclaimed indignantly, "I don't believe you are glad to see me," and throwing her arms around Mrs. Falconer's neck, she strained her closely. "But you poor dear auntie! Come, sit down. I'm going to do all the work now - mine and yours, both. Oh! the beautiful gardening! Rows and rows and rows! With all the other work beside. And me an idle good-for-nothing!"

The two were walking toward a rough bench placed under a tree inside the picket fence. Amy had thrown her arm around Mrs. Falconer's waist.

"But you went to the ball," said the elder woman. "You were not idle there, I imagine. And a ball is good for a great deal. One ought to accomplish more there than in a garden. Besides, you went with John Gray, and he is never idle. Did - he - accomplish - nothing?""Indeed, he was not idle!" exclaimed Amy with a jubilant laugh. "Indeed he did accomplish something - more than he ever did in his life before!"

Mrs. Falconer made no rejoinder; she was too poignantly saying to herself:

"Ah! if it is too late, what will become of him? "

The bench was short. Instinctively they seated themselves as far apart as possible; and they turned their
faces outward across the garden, not toward each other
as they had been used when sitting thus.

The one was nineteen - the tulip: with springlike charm
but perfectly hollow and ready to be filled by east wind
or west wind, north wind or south wind, according as
each blew last and hardest; the other thirty-six - the
rose: in its midsummer splendour with fold upon fold
of delicate symmetric structures, making a
masterpiece.

"Aunt Jessica," Amy began to say drily, as though this
were to be her last concession to a relationship now
about to end, "I might as well tell you everything that
has happened, just as I've been used to doing since I
was a child - when I've done anything wrong." She
gave a faithful story of the carrying off of her party
dress, which of course had been missed and accounted
for, the losing of it and the breaking of her engagement
with John; the return of it and her going to the ball
with Joseph. This brought her mind to the scenes of the
night, and she abandoned herself momentarily to the
delight of reviving them.

"Ah! if you had been there, Aunt Jessica! If they had
seen you in a ball dress as I've seen you without one:
those shoulders! those arms! that skin! You would
have been a swan among the rough-necked, red-necked
turkeys," and Amy glanced a little enviously at a neck
that rose out of the plain dress as though turned by a
sculptor.

The sincere little compliment beat on Mrs. Falconer's ear like a wave upon a stone.

"But if you did not go with John Gray, you danced with him, you talked with him?"

"No," replied Amy, quickly growing grave, "I didn't dance with him. But we talked yes - not much; it was a little too serious for many words," and she sank into a mysterious silence, seeming even to forget herself in some new recess of happiness.

Mrs. Falconer was watching her.

"Ah!" she murmured to herself. "It is too late! too late!" She passed her fingers slowly across her brow with a feeling that life had turned ashen, cold, barren."How is Kitty?" she asked quickly. "Well - as always; and stupid."

"She is always kind and good, isn't she? and faithful."

"Kindness is not always interesting, unfortunately; and goodness is dreadful, and her faithfulness bores me to death."

"At least, she was your hostess, Amy." "I lent her my silk stockings or she'd have had to wear cotton ones," exclaimed Amy, laughing. "We're even."

"If you were merely paying for a lodging, you should have gone to the inn."

"There was nobody at the tavern who could wear my silk stockings; and I had spent all my money."

"Don't you expect Kitty to return your visit?

"I certainly do - more's the pity. She has such big feet!" Amy put out her toe and studied it with vixenish satisfaction.

"Aunt Jessica," she observed at length, looking round at her aunt. "You have to work too hard. And I have always been such a care to you. Wouldn't you like to get rid of me?"

Mrs. Falconer leaned quickly, imploringly, toward her.

"Is that a threat, Amy?"

Amy waited half a minute and then began with a composure that was tinged with condescension:

"You have had so much trouble in your life, Aunt Jessica; so much sorrow."

Mrs. Falconer started and turned upon her niece her eyes that were always exquisite with refinement.

"Amy, have I ever spoken to you of the troubles of my life?" The reproof was majestic in dignity and gentleness.

"You have not."

"Then will you never speak of them to me never again - while you live!"

Amy began again with a dry practical voice, which had in it the sting of revenge; her aunt's rebuke had nettled her.

"At least, I have always been a trouble to you. You sew for me, cook for me, make the garden for me, spin and weave for me, and worry about me. Uncle has to work for me and support me."

The turn of the conversation away from herself brought such relief that Mrs. Falconer replied even warmly.

"You have been a great pleasure to him and to me! The little I have done, you have repaid a thousand fold. Think of us at night without you! Your uncle on one side of the fireplace - me on the other, and you away! Think of us at the table - him at one end, me at the other, and you away! Think of me alone in the house all day, while he is in the fields! Child, I have depended on you - more than you will ever understand!" she added to herself.

"Aunt Jessica," observed Amy with the air of making a fine calculation, "perhaps uncle would think more of you if I were not in the house."

"Amy!"

"Perhaps you would think more of him!"

"Amy!"
"Perhaps if neither of you had me to depend on, you might depend more on each other and be happier."

"You speak to me in this way - on a subject like this! You'd better go!"

"Aunt Jessica," replied Amy, never budging, "the time has been when I would have done so. But it is too late now for you ever to tell me to leave your presence. I am a woman! If I had not been, I shouldn't have said what I just have."

Mrs. Falconer looked at her in silence. This rare gentlewoman had too profound a knowledge of the human heart not to realize that she was completely vanquished. For where in this world is not refinement instantly beaten by coarseness, gentleness by rudeness, all delicacy by all that is indelicate? What can the finest consideration avail against no consideration? the sweetest forbearance against intrusiveness? the beak of the dove against the beak of the hawk? And yet all these may have their victory; for when the finer and the baser metal are forced to struggle with each other in the same field, the finer may always leave it.

With unruffled dignity and with a voice that Amy had never heard - a voice that brought the blood rushing into her cheeks - Mrs. Falconer replied:"Yes; it is true: you are a woman. This is the first day that you have ever made me feel this. For I have always known that as soon as you became one, you would begin to speak to me as you have spoken. I shall never again request you to leave my presence: when it becomes unavoidable, I shall leave yours."

She rose and was moving away. Amy started up and caught her.

"Aunt Jessica, I've something to tell you!" she cried, her face dyed scarlet with the sting.

Mrs. Falconer released herself gently and returned to her seat.

"You know what I mean by what I said?" inquired Amy, still confused but regaining self command rapidly.

"I believe I know: you are engaged to be married."

The words were very faint: they would have reached the subtlest ear with the suggestiveness of a light dreary wind blowing over a desolation.

"Yes; I am engaged to be married."

Amy affirmed it with a definite stress.

"It is this that has made you a woman?

"It is this that has made me a woman."

After the silence of a moment Mrs. Falconer inquired:

"You do not expect to ask my consent - my advice?"

"I certainly do not expect to ask your consent - your advice."

Amy was taking her revenge now - and she always took it as soon as possible.

"Nor your uncle's?"

"Nor my uncle's."

After another, longer silence:

"Do you care to tell me how long this engagement has lasted?"

"Certainly! - Since last night."

"Thank you for telling me that. I think I must go back to my work now."

She walked slowly away. Amy sat still, twirling her bonnet strings and smiling to herself.

This outburst of her new dignity - this initial assertion of her womanhood - had come almost as unexpectedly to herself as to her aunt. She had scarcely known it was in herself to do such a thing. Certain restrictions had been chafing her for a long time: she had not dreamed that they could so readily be set aside, that she had only to stamp her foot violently down on another foot and the other foot would be jerked out of the way. In the flush of elation, she thought of what had just taken place as her Declaration of Independence. She kept on celebrating it in a sort of intoxication at her own audacity:

"I have thrown off the yoke of the Old Dynasty! Glory for the thirteen colonies! A Revolution in half an hour! I'm the mother of a new country! Washington, salute me!"

Then, with perhaps somewhat the feeling of a pullet that has whipped a hen in a barnyard and that after an interval will run all the way across the barnyard to attack again and see whether the victory is complete, she rose and went across the garden, bent on trying the virtue of a final peck.

"But you haven't congratulated me, Aunt Jessica! You have turned your back on the bride elect - you with all your fine manners! She presents herself once more to your notice the future Mrs. Joseph Holden, Junior, to be married one month from last night!" And unexpectedly standing in front of Mrs. Falconer, Amy made one of her low bows which she had practised in the minuet. But catching the sight of the face of her aunt, she cried remorsefully:

"Oh, I have been so rude to you, Aunt Jessica! Forgive me!" There was something of the new sense of womanhood in her voice and of the sisterhood in suffering which womanhood alone can bring.

But Mrs. Falconer had not heard Amy's last exclamation.

"What do you mean?" she asked with quick tremulous eagerness. She had regained her firmness of demeanour, which alone should have turned back any expression of sympathy before it could have been offered.

"That I am to become Mrs. Joseph Holden - a month from last night," repeated Amy bewitchingly.

"You are serious?"

"I am serious!"

Mrs. Falconer did not take Amy's word: she searched her face and eyes with one swift scrutiny that was like a merciless white flame of truth, scorching away all sham, all play, all unreality. Then she dropped her head quickly, so that her own face remained hidden, and silently plied her work. But how the very earth about the rake, how the little roots and clods, seemed to come to life and leap joyously into the air! All at once she dropped everything and came over and took Amy's hand and kissed her cheek. Her lovely eyes were glowing; her face looked as though it had upon it the rosy shadow of the peach trees not far away.

"I do congratulate you," she said sweetly, but with the reserve which Amy's accession to womanhood and the entire conversation of the morning made an unalterable barrier to her. "You have not needed advice: you have chosen wisely. You shall have a beautiful wedding. I will make your dress myself. The like of it will never have been seen in the wilderness. You shall have all the finest linen in the weaving-room. Only a month! How shall we ever get ready! - if we stand idling here! Oh, the work, the work!" she cried and turned to hers with a dismissing smile - unable to trust herself to say more.

"And I must go and take the things out of my bundle," cried Amy, catching the contagion of all this and bounding away to the house. Some five minutes later Mrs. Falconer glanced at the sun: it was eleven o'clock - time to be getting dinner.

When she reached her room, Amy was standing beside the bed, engaged in lifting out of the bundle the finery now so redolent of the ball. "Aunt Jessica," she remarked carelessly, without looking round, "I forgot to tell you that John Gray had a fight with a panther in his schoolroom this morning," and she gave several gossamer-like touches to the white lace tucker. Mrs. Falconer had seated herself in a chair to rest. She had taken off her bonnet, and her fingers were unconsciously busy with the lustrous edges of her heavy hair. At Amy's words her hands fell to her lap. But she had long ago learned the value of silence and self-control when she was most deeply moved: Amy had already surprised her once that morning.

"The panther bit him in the shoulder close to the neck," continued Amy, folding the tucker away and lifting out the blue silk coat. "They were on the floor of the school-house in the last struggle when Erskine got there. He had gone for Phoebe Lovejoy's cows, because it was raining and she couldn't go herself; and he heard John as he was passing. He said his voice sounded like the bellow of a dying bull." "Is he much hurt? Where is he? Did you go to see him? ho dressed his wound? Who is with him?"

"They carried him home," said Amy, turning round to the light and pressing the beautiful silk coat in against her figure with little kicks at the skirt. "No; I didn't go; Joseph came round and told me. He didn't think the wound was very dangerous - necessarily. One of his hands was terribly clawed."

"A panther? In town? In his schoolroom?" -

"You know Erskine keeps a pet panther. I heard him tell Mrs. Poythress it was a female," said Amy with an apologetic icy, knowing little laugh. "And he said this one had been prowling about in the edge of the canebrakes for several days. He had been trying to get a shot at it. He says it was nearly starved: that was why it wanted to eat John whole before breakfast."

Amy turned back to the bed and shook out delicately the white muslin dress - the dress that John had hung on the wall of his cabin - that had wound itself around his figure so clingingly.

There was silence in the room. Amy had now reached the silk stockings; and taking up one, she blew down into it and quickly peeped over the side, to see whether it would fill out to life-size - with a mischievous wink.

"I am going to him at once."

Amy looked up in amazement. "But, Aunt Jessica," she observed reproachfully; "who will get uncle's dinner? You know I can't." "Tell your uncle what has happened as soon as he comes."

She had risen and was making some rapid preparations.

"I want my dinner," said Amy ruefully, seating herself on the edge of the bed and watching her aunt with disapproval.

"You can't go now!" she exclaimed. "Uncle has the horses in the field."

Mrs. Falconer turned to her with simple earnestness.

"I hoped you would lend me your horse?"

"But he is tired; and beside I want to use him this afternoon: Kitty and I are going visiting."

"Tell your uncle when he comes in," said Mrs. Falconer, turning in the doorway a minute later, and speaking rapidly to her niece, but without the least reproach, "tell your uncle that his friend is badly hurt. Tell him that we do not know how badly. Tell him that I have gone to find out and to do anything for him that

I can. Tell him to follow me at once. He will find me at his bedside. I am sorry about the dinner."

XII

SEVERAL days had slipped by.

At John's request they had moved his bed across the doorway of his cabin; and stretched there, he could see the sun spring every morning out the dimpled emerald ocean of the wilderness; and the moon follow at night, silvering the soft ripples of the multitudinous leaves lapping the shores of silence: days when the inner noises of life sounded like storms; nights when everything within him lay as still as memory.

His wounds had behaved well from the out-set. When he had put forth all his frenzied despairing strength to throttle the cougar, it had let go its hold only to sink its fangs more deeply into his flesh, thus increasing the laceration; and there was also much laceration of the hand. But the rich blood flowing in him was the purest; and among a people who for a quarter of a century had been used to the treatment of wounds, there prevailed a rough but genuine skill that stood him in good stead. To these hardy fighting folk, as to him, it was a scratch and he would have liked to go on with his teaching. Warned of the danger of inflammation, however, he took to his bed; and according to our own nervous standards which seem to have intensified pain for us beyond the comprehension of our forefathers, he was sick and a great sufferer.

Those long cool, sweet, brilliant days! Those long still, lonely, silvery nights! His cabin stood near the crest of the hill that ran along the southern edge of the settlement; and propped on his bed, he could look down into the wide valley - into the town. The frame of his door became the frame of many a living picture. Under a big shady tree at the creek-side, he could see some of his children playing or fishing: their shouts and laughter were borne to his ear; he could recognize their shrill voices - those always masterful voices of boys at their games. Sometimes these little figures were framed timidly just outside the door - the girls with small wilted posies, the boys with inquiries. But there was no disguising the dread they all felt that he might soon be well: he had felt himself once; he did not blame them. Wee Jennie even came up with her slate one day and asked him to set her a sum in multiplication; he did so; but he knew that she would rub it out as soon as she could get out of sight, and he laughed quietly to himself at this tiny casuist, who was trying so hard to deceive them both.

Two or three times, now out in the sunlight, now under the shadow of the trees, he saw an old white horse go slowly along the distant road; and a pink skirt and a huge white bonnet - two or three times; but he watched for it a thousand times till his eyes grew weary.

One day Erskine brought the skin of the panther which he was preparing for him, to take the place of the old one under his table. He brought his rifle along also, - his "Betsy," as he always called it; which, however, he declared was bewitched just now; and for a while John watched him curiously as he nailed a target on a tree in front of John's door, drew on it the face of the person whom he charged with having bewitched his gun, and then, standing back, shot it with a silver bullet; after which, the spell being now undone, he dug the bullet out of the tree again and went off to hunt with confidence in his luck.

And then the making of history was going on under his eyes down there in the town, and many a thoughtful hour he studied that. The mere procession of figures across his field of vision symbolized the march of destiny, the onward sweep of the race, the winning of the continent. Now the barbaric paint and plumes of some proud Indian, peaceably come to trade in pelts but really to note the changes that had taken place in his great hunting ground, loved and ranged of old beyond all others: this figure was the Past - the old, old Past. Next, the picturesque, rugged outlines of some backwoods rifleman, who with his fellows had dislodged and pushed the Indian westward: this figure was the Present - the short-lived Present. Lastly, dislodging this figure in turn and already pushing him westward as he had driven the Indian, a third type of historic man, the fixed settler, the land-loving, house-building, wife-bringing, child-getting, stock-breeding yeoman of the new field and pasture: this was the figure of the endless Future. The retreating wave of Indian life, the thin restless wave of frontier life, the on-coming, all-burying wave of civilized life - he seemed to feel close to him the mighty movements of the three. His own affair, the attack of the panther, the last encounter between the cabin and the jungle looked to him as typical of the conquest; and that he should have come out of the struggle alive, and have owed his life to the young Indian fighter and hunter who had sprung between him and the incarnate terror of the wilderness, affected his imagination as an epitome of the whole winning of the West.

James Lane Allen

One morning while the earth was still fresh with dew, the great Boone came to inquire for him, and before he left, drew from the pocket of his hunting shirt a well-worn little volume.

"It has been my friend many a night," he said. "I have read it by many a camp-fire. I had it in my pocket when I stood on the top of Indian Old Fields and saw the blue grass lands for the first time. And when we encamped on the creek there, I named it Lulbegrud in honour of my book. You can read it while you have nothing else to do;" and he astounded John by leaving in his hand Swift's story of adventures in new worlds.

He had many other visitors: the Governor, Mr. Bradford, General Wilkinson, the leaders in the French movement, all of whom were solicitous for his welfare as a man, but also as their chosen emissary to the Jacobin Club of Philadelphia. In truth it seemed to him that everyone in the town came sooner or later, to take a turn at his bedside or wish him well.

Except four persons: Amy did not come; nor Joseph, with whom he had quarrelled and with whom he meant to settle his difference as soon as he could get about; nor O'Bannon, whose practical joke had indirectly led to the whole trouble; nor Peter, who toiled on at his forge with his wounded vanity.

Betrothals were not kept secret in those days and engagements were short. But as he was sick and suffering, some of those who visited him forbore to mention her name, much less to speak of the preparations now going forward for her marriage with Joseph. Others, indeed, did begin to talk of her and to pry; but he changed the subject quickly.

And so he lay there with the old battle going on in his thoughts, never knowing that she had promised to become the wife of another: fighting it all over in his foolish, iron-minded way: some days hardening and saying he would never look her in the face again; other days softening and resolving to seek her out as soon as he grew well enough and learn whether the fault of all this quarrel lay with him or wherein lay the truth: yet in all his moods sore beset with doubts of her sincerity and at all times passing sore over his defeat - defeat that always went so hard with him.

Meantime one person was pondering his case with a solicitude that he wist not of: the Reverend James Moore, the flute-playing Episcopal parson of the town, within whose flock this marriage was to take place and who may have regarded Amy as one of his most frisky wayward fleeces. Perhaps indeed as not wearing a white spiritual fleece at all but as dyed a sort of merino-brown in the matter of righteousness.

He had long been fond of John - they both being pure-minded men, religious, bookish, and bachelors; but their friendship caused one to think of the pine and the palm: for the parson, with his cold bleak face, palish straight hair put back behind white ears, and frozen smile, appeared always to be inhabiting the arctic regions of life while John, though rooted in a tropical soil of many passions, strove always to bear himself in character like a palm, up-right, clean-cut; having no low or drooping branches; and putting forth all the foliage and blossoms of the mind at the very summit of his powers. The parson and the school-master had often walked out to the Falconers' together in the days when John imagined his suit to be faring prosperously; and from Amy's conduct, and his too slight knowledge of the sex, this arctic explorer had long since adjusted his frosted faculties to the notion that she expected to become John's wife. He was sorry; it sent an extra chill through the icebergs of his imagination; but perhaps he gathered comforting warmth from the hope that some of John's whiteness would fall upon her and that thus from being a blackish lambkin she would at least eventually turn into a light-gray ewe.

When the tidings reached his far-inward ear that she was to marry Joseph instead of his friend, a general thaw set in over the entire landscape of his nature: it was like spring along the southern fringes of Greenland.

The error must not be inculcated here that the parson had no passions: he had three-ruling ones: a passion for music, a passion for metaphysics, and a passion for satirizing the other sex.

Dropping in one afternoon and glancing with delicate indirection at John's short shelf of books, he inquired whether he had finished with his Paley. John said he had and the parson took it down to bear away with him. Laying it across his stony knees as he sat down and piling his white hands on it,

"Do you believe Paley?" he asked, turning upon John a pair of the most beautiful eyes, which looked a little like moss agates.

"I believe St. Paul," replied John, turning his own eyes fondly on his open Testament.

"Do you believe Paley?" insisted the parson, who would always have his questions answered directly.

"There's a good deal of Paley: what do you mean?" said John, laughing evasively.

"I mean his ground idea-the corner stone of his doctrine -his pou sto. I mean do you believe that we can infer the existence and character of God from any evidences of design that we see in the universe "

"I'm not so sure about that," said John. "What we call the evidences of design in the universe may be merely certain laws of our own minds, certain inward necessities we are under to think of everything as having an order and a plan and a cause. And these inner necessities may themselves rest on nothing, may be wrong, may be deceiving us."

"Oh, I don't mean that!" said the parson. "We've got to believe our own minds. We've got to do that even to disbelieve them. If the mind says of itself it is a liar, how does it know this to be true if it is a liar itself? No; we have to believe our own minds whether they are right or wrong. But what I mean is: can we, according to Paley, infer the existence and character of God from anything we see?" "It sounds reasonable," said John. "Does it! Then suppose you apply this method of reasoning to a woman: can you infer her existence from anything you see? Can you trace the evidences of design there? Can you derive the slightest notion of her character from her works?" As the parson said this, he turned upon the sick man a look of such logical triumph that John, who for days had been wearily trying to infer Amy's character from what she had done, was seized with a fit of laughter - the parson himself remaining perfectly grave.

Another day he examined John's wound tenderly, and

then sat down by him with his beautiful moss-agate eyes emitting dangerous little sparkles.

"It's a bad bite," he said, "the bite of a cat - felis concolor. They are a bad family - these cats - the scratchers." He was holding John's wounded hand. "So you've had your fight with a felis. A single encounter ought to be enough! If some one hadn't happened to step in and save you! - What do you suppose is the root of the idea universal in the consciousness of our race that if a man had not been a man he'd have been a lion; and that if a woman hadn't been a woman she'd have been a tigress? "

"I don't believe there's any such idea universal in the consciousness of the race," replied John, laughing.

"It's universal in my consciousness," said the parson doggedly, "and my consciousness is as valid as any other man's. But I'll ask you an easier question: who of all men, do you suppose, knew most about women?"

"Women or Woman?" inquired John.

"Women," said the parson. "We'll drop the subject of Woman: she's beyond us!

"I don't know," observed John. "St. Paul knew a good deal, and said some necessary things."

"St. Paul!" exclaimed the parson condescendingly. "He knew a few noble Jewesses - superficially - with a scattering acquaintance among the pagan sisters around the shores of the Mediterranean. As for what he wrote on that subject - it may have been inspired by Heaven: it never could have been inspired by the sex."

"Shakspeare, I suppose," said John. "The man in the Arabian Nights," cried the parson, who may have been put in mind of this character by his own attempts to furnish daily entertainment. "He knew a thousand of them - intimately. And cut off the heads of nine hundred and ninety-nine! The only reason he did not cut off the head of the other was that he had learned enough: he could not endure to know any more. All the evidence had come in: the case was closed."

"I suppose there are men in the world," he continued, "who would find it hard to stand a single disappointment about a woman. But think of a thousand disappointments! A thousand attempts to find a good wife - just one woman who could furnish a man a little rational companionship at night. Bluebeard also must have been a well-informed person. And Henry the Eighth - there was a man who had evidently picked up considerable knowledge and who made considerable use of it. But to go back a moment to the idea of the felis family. Suppose we do this: we'll begin to enumerate the qualities of the common house cat. I'll think of the cat; you think of some woman; and we'll see what we come to."

"I'll not do it," said John. "She's too noble."

"Just for fun!"

"There's no fun in comparing a woman to a cat."

"There is if she doesn't know it. Come, begin!" And the parson laid one long forefinger on one long little finger and waited for the first specification. "Fineness," said John, thinking of a certain woman.

"Fondness for a nap," said the parson, thinking of a certain cat.

"Grace," said John.
"Inability to express thanks," said the parson.

"A beautiful form," said John."A desire to be stroked," said the parson. "Sympathy," said John. "Oh, no!" said the parson; "no cat has any sympathy. A dog has: a man is more of a dog." "Noble-mindedness," said John.

"That will not do either," said the parson. "Cats are not noble-minded; it's preposterous!"

"Perfect case of manner," said John.

"Perfect indifference of manner," said the parson."

"No vanity," said John. "No sense of humour," said the parson.

"Plenty of wit," said John.

"You keep on thinking too much about some woman," remonstrated the parson, slightly exasperated.

"Fastidiousness," said John.

"Soft hands and beautiful nails," said the parson, nodding encouragingly.

"A gentle footstep," said John with a softened look coming into his eyes. "A quiet presence."

"Beautiful taste in music," said John.

"Oh! dreadful!" said the parson. "What on earth are you thinking about?"

"The love of rugs and cushions," said John, groping desperately. "The love of a lap," said the parson fluently.

"The love of playing with its victim," said John, thinking of another woman.

"Capital!" cried the parson. "That's the truest thing we've said. We'll not spoil it by another word;" but he searched John's face covertly to see whether this talk had beguiled him.

All this satire meant nothing sour, or bitter, or ignoble with the parson. It was merely the low, far-off play of the northern lights of his mind, irradiating the long polar night of his bachelorhood. But even on the polar night the sun rises - a little way; and the time came when he married - as one might expect to find the flame of a volcano hidden away in a mountain of Iceland spar.

Toward the end of his illness, John lay one night inside his door, looking soberly, sorrowfully out into the moonlight. A chair sat outside, and the parson walked quietly up the green hill and took it. Then he laid his hat on the grass; and passed his delicate hands slowly backward over his long fine straight hair, on which the moonbeams at once fell with a luster as upon still water or the finest satin.

They talked awhile of the best things in life, as they commonly did. At length the parson said in his unworldly way:

"I have one thing against Aristotle: he said the effect of the flute was bad and exciting. He was no true Greek. John, have you ever thought how much of life can be expressed in terms of music? To me every civilization has given out its distinct musical quality; the ages have their peculiar tones; each century its key, its scale. For generations in Greece you can hear nothing but the pipes; during other generations nothing but the lyre. Think of the long, long time among the Romans when your ear is reached by the trumpet alone.

"Then again whole events in history come down to me with the effect of an orchestra, playing in the distance; single lives sometimes like a great solo. As for the people I know or have known, some have to me the sound of brass, some the sound of wood, some the sound of strings. Only - so few, so very, very few yield the perfect music of their kind. The brass is a little too loud; the wood a little too muffled; the strings - some of the strings are invariably broken. I know a big man who is nothing but a big drum; and I know another whose whole existence has been a jig on a fiddle; and I know a shrill little fellow who is a fife; and I know a brassy girl who is a pair of cymbals; and once - once," repeated the parson whimsically, "I knew an old maid who was a real living spinet. I even know another old maid now who is nothing but an old music book - long ago sung through, learned by heart, and laid aside: in a faded, wrinkled binding - yellowed paper stained by tears - and haunted by an odour of rose-petals, crushed between the leaves of memory: a genuine very thin and stiff collection of the rarest original songs - not songs without words, but songs without sounds - the ballads of an undiscovered heart, the hymns of an unanswered spirit."

After a pause during which neither of the men spoke, the parson went on:

"All Ireland - it is a harp! We know what Scotland is. John," he exclaimed, suddenly turning toward the dark figure lying just inside the shadow, "you are a discord of the bagpipe and the harp: there's the trouble with you. Sometimes I can hear the harp alone in you, and then I like you; but when the bagpipe begins, you are worse than a big bumblebee with a bad cold."

"I know it," said John sorrowfully. "My only hope is that the harp will outlast the bee."

"At least that was a chord finely struck," said the parson warmly. After another silence he went on.

"Martin Luther - he was a cathedral organ. And so it goes. And so the whole past sounds to me: it is the music of the world: it is the vast choir of the ever-living dead." He gazed dreamily up at the heavens: "Plato! he is the music of the stars."

After a little while, bending over and looking at the earth and speaking in a tone of unconscious humility, he added:

"The most that we can do is to begin a strain that will swell the general volume and last on after we have perished. As for me, when I am gone, I should like the memory of my life to give out the sound of a flute."

He slipped his hand softly into the breastpocket of his coat and more softly drew something out.

" Would you like a little music?" he asked shyly, his

cold beautiful face all at once taking on an expression of angelic sweetness.

John quickly reached out and caught his hand in a long, crushing grip: he knew this was the last proof the parson could ever have given him that he loved him. And then as he lay back on his pillow, he turned his face back into the dark cabin.

Out upon the stillness of the night floated the parson's passion - silver-clear, but in an undertone of such peace, of such immortal gentleness. It was as though the very beams of the far-off serenest moon, falling upon his flute and dropping down into its interior through its little round openings, were by his touch shorn of all their lustre, their softness, their celestial energy, and made to reissue as music. It was as though his flute had been stuffed with frozen Alpine blossoms and these had been melted away by the passionate breath of his soul into the coldest invisible flowers of sound. At last, as though all these blossoms in his flute had been used up - blown out upon the warm, moon-lit air as the snow-white fragrances of the ear - the parson buried his face softly upon his elbow which rested on the back of his chair. And neither man spoke again.

XIII

WHEN Mrs. Falconer had drawn near John's hut on the morning of his misfortune, it was past noon despite all her anxious, sorrowful haste to reach him. His wounds had been dressed. The crowd of people that had gathered about his cabin were gone back to their occupations or their homes - except a group that sat on the roots of a green tree several yards from his door. Some of these were old wilderness folk living near by who had offered to nurse him and otherwise to care for his comforts and needs. The affair furnished them that renewed interest in themselves which is so liable to revisit us when we have escaped a fellow-creature's suffering but can relate good things about ourselves in like risks and dangers; and they were drawing out their reminiscences now with unconscious gratitude for so excellent an opportunity befalling them in these peaceful unadventurous days. Several of John's boys lay in the grass and hung upon these narratives. Now and then they cast awe-stricken glances at his door which had been pushed to, that he might be quiet; or, if his pain would let him, drop into a little sleep. They made it their especial care, when any new-comer hurried past, to arrest him with the command that he must not go in; and they would thus have stopped Mrs. Falconer but she put them gently aside without heed or hearing.

When she softly pushed the door open, John was not asleep. He lay in a corner on his low hard bed of skins against the wall of logs - his eyes wide open, the hard white glare of the small shutter-less window falling on his face. He turned to her the look of a dumb animal that can say nothing of why it has been wounded or of how it is suffering; stretched out his hand gratefully; and drew her toward him. She sat down on the edge of the bed, folded her quivering fingers across his temples, smoothed back his heavy, coarse, curling hair, and bending low over his eyes, rained down into them the whole unuttered, tearless passion of her distress, her sympathy. Major Falconer came for her within the hour and she left with him almost as soon as he arrived. When she was gone, John lay thinking of her.

"What a nurse she is!" he said, remembering how she had concerned herself solely his about life, his safety, his wounds. Once she had turned quickly:

"Now you can't go away!" she had said with a smile that touched him deeply.

"I wish you didn't have to go!" he had replied mourningfully, feeling his sudden dependence on her.

This was the first time she had ever been in room - with its poverty, its bareness. She must have cast about it a look of delicate inquiry - as a woman is apt to do in a singleman's abode; for when she came again, in addition to pieces of soft old linen for bandages brought fresh cool fragrant sheets - the work of her own looms; a better pillow with a pillow-case on it that was delicious to his cheek; for he had his weakness about clean, white linen. She put a curtain over the pitiless window. He saw a wild rose in a glass beside his Testament. He discovered moccasin slippers beside his bed.

"And here," she had said just before leaving, with her hand on a pile of things and with an embarrassed laugh - keeping her face turned away - "here are some towels." Under the towels he found two night shirts - new ones.

When she was gone, he lay thinking of her again.

He had gratefully slipped on one of the shirts. He was feeling the new sense of luxury that is imparted by a bed enriched with snow-white, sweet-smelling pillows and sheets. The curtain over his window strained into his room a light shadowy, restful. The flower on his table, - the transforming touch in his room - her noble brooding tenderness - everything went into his gratitude, his remembrance of her. But all this - he argued with a sudden taste for fine discrimination - had not been done out of mere anxiety for his life: it was not the barren solicitude of a nurse but the deliberate, luxurious regard of a mother for his comfort: no doubt it represented the ungovernable overflow of the maternal, long pent-up in her ungratified. And by this route he came at last to a thought of her that novel for him - the pitying recollection of her childlessness.

"What a mother she would have been!" he said rebelliously. "The mother of sons who would have become great through her - and greater through the memory of her after she was gone." When she came again, seeing him out of danger and seeing him comfortable, she seated herself beside his table and opened her work."It isn't good for you to talk much," she soon said reprovingly, "and I have to work - and to think."

And so he lay watching her - watching her beautiful
fingers which never seemed to rest in life - watching
her quiet brow with its ripple of lustrous hair forever
suggesting to him how her lovely neck and shoulders
would be buried by it if its long light waves were but
loosened. To have a woman sitting by his table with
her sewing - it turned his room into something vaguely
dreamed of heretofore: a home. She finished a sock for
Major Falconer and began on one of his shirts. He
counted the stitches as they went into a sleeve. They
made him angry. And her face! - over it had come a
look of settled weariness; for perhaps if there is ever a
time when a woman forgets and the inward sorrow
steals outward to the surface as an unwatched shadow
along a wall, it is when she sews.

"What a wife she is!" he reflected enviously after she
was gone; and he tried not to think of certain matters in
her life. "What a wife! How unfaltering in duty!"

The next time she came, it was early. She seemed to
him to have bathed in the freshness, the beauty, the
delight of the morning. He had never seen her so
radiant, so young. She was like a woman who holds in
her hand the unopened casket of life - its jewels still
ungazed on, still unworn. There was some secret
excitement in her as though the moment had at last
come for her to open it. She had but a few moments to
spare.

"I have brought you a book," she said, smiling and
laying her cheek against a rose newly placed by his
Testament. For a moment she scrutinized him with
intense penetration. Then she added:

"Will you read it wisely?"

"I will if I am wise," he replied laughing. "Thank you," and he held out his hand for the book eagerly. She clasped it more tightly with the gayest laugh of irresolution. Her colour deepened. A moment later, however, she recovered the simple and noble seriousness to which she had grown used as the one habit of her life with him.

"You should have read it long ago," she said. "But it is not too late for you. Perhaps now is your best time. It is a good book for a man, wounded as you have been; and by the time you are well, you will need it more than you have ever done. Hereafter you will always need it more."

She spoke with partly hidden significance, as one who knows life may speak to one who does not. He eyed the book despairingly.

"It is my old Bible of manhood," she continued with rich soberness, " part worthless, part divine. Not Greek manhood - nor Roman manhood: they were too pagan. Not Semitic manhood: that - in its ideal at least - was not pagan enough. But something better than any of these - something that is everything." The subject struck inward to the very heart's root of his private life. He listened as with breath arrested.

"We know what the Greeks were before everything else," she said resolutely: " hey were physical men: we think less of them spiritually in any sense of the idea that is valued by us and of course we do not think of them at all as gentlemen: that involves of course the highest courtesy to women. The Jews were of all things spiritual in the type of their striving. Their ancient system, and the system of the New Testament itself as it was soon taught and passed down to us, struck a deadly blow at the development of the body for its own sake - at physical beauty: and the highest development of the body is what the race can never do without. It struck another blow at the development of taste - at the luxury and grace of the intellect: which also the race can never do without. But in this old book you will find the starting-point of a new conception of ideal human life. It grew partly out of the pagan; it grew partly out of the Christian; it added from its own age something of its own. Nearly every nation of Europe has lived on it ever since - as its ideal. The whole world is being nourished by that ideal more and more. It is the only conception of itself that the race can never fall away from without harm, because it is the ideal of its own perfection. You know what I mean?" she asked a little imperiously as though she were talking to a green boy.

"What do you mean?" he asked wonderingly. She had never spoken to him in this way. Her mood, the passionate, beautiful, embarrassed stress behind all this, was a bewildering revelation.

"I mean," she said, "that first of all things in this world a man must be a man - with all the grace and vigour and, if possible, all the beauty of the body. Then he must be a gentleman - with all the grace, the vigour, the good taste of the mind. And then with both of these - no matter what his creed, his dogmas, his superstitions, his religion - with both of these he must try to live a beautiful life of the spirit." He looked at her eagerly, gratefully.

"You will find him all these," she resumed, dropping her eyes before his gratitude which was much too personal. "You will find all these in this book: here are men who were men; here are men who were gentlemen; and here are gentlemen who served the unfallen life of the spirit."

She kept her eyes on the book. Her voice had become very grave and reverent. She had grown more embarrassed, but at last she went on as though resolved to finish:

"So it ought to help you! It will help you. It will help you to be what you are trying to be. There are things here that you have sought and have never found. There are characters here whom you have wished to meet without ever having known that they existed. If you will always live by what is best in this book, love the best that it loves, hate what it hates, scorn what it scorns, follow its ideals to the end of the world, to the end of your life - "

"Oh, but give it to me!" he cried, lifting himself impulsively on one elbow and holding out his hand for it. She came silently over to the bedside and placed it on his hand. He studied the title wonderingly, wonderingly turned some of the leaves, and at last, smiling with wonder still, looked up at her. And then he forgot the book - forgot everything but her.

Once upon a time he had been walking along a woodland path with his eyes fixed on the ground in front of him as was his studious wont. In the path itself there had not been one thing to catch his notice: only brown dust - little stones - a twig - some blades of withered grass.

Then all at once out of this dull, dead motley of harmonious nothingness, a single gorgeous spot had revealed itself, swelled out, and disappeared: a butterfly had opened its wings, laid bare their inside splendours, and closed them again - presenting to the eye only the adaptive, protective, exterior of those marvellous swinging doors of its life. He had wondered then that Nature could so paint the two sides of this thinnest of all canvases: the outside merely daubed over that it might resemble the dead and common and worthless things amid which the creature had to live - a masterwork of concealment; the inside designed and drawn and coloured with lavish fullness of plan, grace of curve, marvel of hue - all for the purpose of the exquisite self revelation which should come when the one great invitation of existence was sought or was given. As the young school-master now looked up - too quickly - at the woman who stood over him, her eyes were like a butterfly's gorgeous wings that for an instant had opened upon him and already were closing - closing upon the hidden splendours of her nature - closing upon the power to receive upon walls of beauty all the sunlight of the world.

"What a woman!" he said to himself, strangely troubled a moment later when she was gone. He had not looked at the book again. It lay forgotten by his pillow.

"What a woman!" he repeated, with a sigh that was like a groan.

Her bringing of the book - her unusual conversation - her excitement - her seriousness - the impression she made upon him that a new problem was beginning to work itself out in her life - most of all that one startling revelation of herself at the instant of turning away: all these occupied his thoughts that day.

She did not return the next or the next or the next. And, it was during these long vacant hours that he began to weave curiously together all that he had ever heard of her and of her past; until, in the end, he accomplished something like a true restoration of her life - in the colour of his own emotions. Then he fell to wandering up and down this long vista of scenes as he might have sought unwearied secret gallery of pictures through which he alone had the privilege of walking.

At the far end of the vista he could behold her in her childhood as the daughter of a cavalier land-holder in the valley of the James: an heiress of a vast estate with its winding creeks and sunny bays, its tobacco plantations worked by troops of slaves, its deer parks and open country for the riding to hounds. There was the manor-house in the style of the grand places of the English gentry from whom her father was descended; sloping from the veranda to the river landing a wide lawn covered with the silvery grass of the English parks, its walks bordered with hedges of box, its summer-house festooned with vines, its terraces gay with the old familiar shrubs and flowers loyally brought over from the mother land. He could see her as, some bright summer morning, followed by a tame fawn, she bounded down the lawn to the private landing where a slow frigate had stopped to break bulk on its way to Williamsburg-perhaps to put out with other furniture a little mahogany chair brought especially for herself over the rocking sea from London or where some round-sterned packet from New England or New Amsterdam was unloading its cargo of grain or hides or rum in exchange for her father's tobacco. Perhaps to greet her father himself returning from a long absence amid old scenes that still could draw him back to England; or standing lonely on the pier, to watch in tears him and her brothers - a vanishing group - as they waved her a last good-bye and drifted slowly out to the blue ocean on their way "home" to school at Eton.

He liked to dwell on the picture of her as a little school-girl herself: sent fastidiously on her way, with long gloves covering her arms, a white linen mask tied over her face to screen her complexion from tan, a sunbonnet sewed tightly on her head to keep it secure from the capricious winds of heaven and the more variable gusts of her own wilfulness; or on another picture of her - as a lonely little lass - begging to be taken to court, where she could marvel at her father, an awful judge in his wig and his robe of scarlet and black velvet; or on a third picture of her - as when she was marshalled into church behind a liveried servant bearing the family prayer-book, sat in the raised pew upholstered in purple velvet, with its canopy overhead and the gilt letters of the family name in front; and a little farther away on the wall of the church the Lord's Prayer and the Commandments put there by her father at the cost of two thousand pounds of his best tobacco; finally to be preached to by a minister with whom her father sometimes spilt wine on the table-cloth, and who had once fought a successful duel behind his own sanctuary of peace and good will to all men. Here succeeded other scenes; for as his interest deepened, he never grew tired of this restorative image-building by which she could be brought always more vividly before his imagination.

Her childhood gone , then , he followed her as she

glided along the shining creeks from plantation to plantation in a canoe manned by singing black oarsmen: or rode abroad followed by her greyhound, her face concealed by a black velvet riding mask kept in place by a silver mouth-piece held between her teeth; or when autumn waned, went rolling slowly along towards Williamsburg or Annapolis in the great family coach of mahogany, with its yellow facings, Venetian windows, projection lamps, and high seat for footmen and coachman - there to take a house for the winter season - there to give and to be given balls, where she trod the minuet, stiff in blue brocade, her white shoulders rising out of a bodice hung with gems, her beautiful head bearing aloft its tower of long white feathers. Yet with most of her life passed at the great lonely country-house by the bright river: qazing wistfully out of the deep-mullioned windows of diamond panes; flitting up and down the wide staircase of carven oak; buried in its library, with its wainscoted walls crossed with swords and hung with portraits of soldierly faces: all of which pleased him best, he being a home-lover. So that when facts were lacking, sometimes he would kindle true fancies of her young life in this place: as when she reclined on mats and cushions in the breeze-swept balls, fanned by a slave and reading the Tatler or the Spectator; or if it were the chill twilights of October, perhaps came in from a walk in the cool woods with a red leaf at her white throat, and seated herself at the spinet, while a low blaze from the deep chimney seat flickered over her face, and the low music flickered with the shadows; or when the white tempests of winter raved outside, gave her nights to the reading of "Tom Jones," by the light of myrtleberry candles on a slender-legged mahogany table.

James Lane Allen

But he had heard a great deal of her visits at the other great country places of the day. Often at Greenway Court, where her father went to ride to hounds with Lord Fairfax and Washington; at Carter's Grove; at the homes of the Berkeleys, the Masons, the Spottswoods; once, indeed, at Castlewood itself, where the stately Madam Esmond Warrington had placed her by her own side at dinner and had kissed her check at leaving; but oftenest at Brandon Mansion where one of her heroines had lived - Evelyn Byrd; so that, Sir Godfrey Knell having painted that sad young lady, who now lies with a heavy stone on her heavier heart in the dim old burying-ground at Westover, she would have it that hers must be painted in the same identical fashion, with herself sitting on a green bank, a cluster of roses in her hand, a shepherd's crook across her knees.

And then, just as she was fairly opening into the earliest flower of womanhood, the sudden, awful end of all this half-barbaric, half-aristocratic life - the revolt of the colonies, the outbreak of the Revolution, the blaze of way that swept the land like a forest fire, and that enveloped in its furies even the great house on the James. One of her brothers turned Whig, and already gone impetuously away in his uniform of buff and blue, to follow the fortunes of Washington; the other siding with the "home" across the sea, and he too already ridden impetuously away in scarlet. Her proud father, his heart long torn between these two and between his two countries, pacing the great hall, his face flushed with wine, his eyes turning confusedly, pitifully, on the soldierly portraits of his ancestors; until at last he too was gone, to keep his sword and his conscience loyal to his king.

And then more dreadful years and still sadder times; as

when one dark morning toward daybreak, by the edge of a darker forest draped with snow where the frozen dead lay thick, they found an officer's hat half filled with snow, and near by, her father fallen face downward; and turning him over, saw a bullet-hole over his breast, and the crimson of his blood on the scarlet of his waistcoat; so departed, with manfulness out of this world and leaving behind him some finer things than his debts and mortgages over dice and cards and dogs and wine and lotteries. Then not long after that, the manor-house on the James turned into the unkindest of battlefields; one brother defending at the head of troops within, the other attacking at the head of troops without; the snowy bedrooms becoming the red-stained wards of a hospital; the staircase hacked by swords; the poor little spinet and the slender-legged little mahogany tables overturned and smashed, the portraits slashed, the library scattered. Then one night, seen from a distance, a vast flame licking the low clouds; and afterwards a black ruin where the great house had stood, and so the end of it all forever.

During these years, she, herself, had been like a lily in a lake, never uprooted, but buried out of sight beneath the storm that tosses the waves back and forth.

Then white and heavenly Peace again, and the liberty of the Anglo-Saxon race in the New World. But with wounds harder to heal than those of the flesh; with memories that were as sword-points broken off in the body; with glory to brighten more and more, as time went on, but with starvation close at hand. Virginia willing to pay her heroes but having naught wherewith to pay, until the news comes from afar, that while all this has been going on in the East, in the West the rude border-folk, the backwoodsmen of the Blue Ridge and the Alleghanies, without generals, without commands, without help or pay, or reward of any kind, but fighting of their own free will and dyeing every step of their advance with their blood, had entered and conquered the great neutral game-park of the Northern and the Southern Indians, and were holding it against all plots: in the teeth of all comers and against the frantic Indians themselves; against England, France, Spain, - a new land as good as the best of old England - Kentucky! Into which already thousands upon thousands were hurrying in search of homes - a new movement of the race - its first spreading-out over the mighty continent upon its mightier destiny.

So had come about her hasty marriage with her young officer, whom Virginia rewarded for his service with land; so had followed the breaking of all ties, to journey by his side into the wilderness, there to undergo hardship, perhaps death itself after captivity and torture such that no man who has ever loved a woman can even look another man in the face and name.

Thus ever on and on unwittingly he wove the fibres of her life about him as his shirt of destiny: following the threads nearer, always nearer, toward the present, until he reached the day on which he had first met her on his in the wilderness. From that time, he no longer relied upon hearsay, but drew from his own knowledge of her to fill out and so far to end all these fond tapestries of his memory and imagination.

But as one who has traversed a long gallery of pictures, and, turning to look back upon all that he has passed, sees a straight track narrowing away into the dimming distance, and only the last few life scenes standing out lustrous and clear, so the school-master, gazing down this long vista, beheld at the far end of it a little girl, whom he did not know, playing on the silvery ancestral lawns of the James; at the near end, watching by his bedside on this rude border of the West, a woman who had become indispensable to his friendship.

More days passed, and still she did not return. His eagerness for her rose and followed, and sorrowfully set with every sun.

Meantime he read the book, beginning it with an effort through finding it hard to withdraw his mind from his present. But soon he was clutching it with a forgotten hand and lay on his bed for hours joined fast to it with unreleasing eyes; draining its last words into his heart, with a thirst newly begotten and growing always the more quenchless as it was always being quenched. So that having finished it, he read it again, now seeing the high end of it all from the low beginning. And then a third time, more clingingly, more yearningly yet, thrice lighting the fire in his blood with the same straw. Like a vital fire it was left in him at last, a red and white of flame; the two flames forever hostile, and seeking each to burn the other out. And while it stayed in him thus as a fire, it had also filled all tissues of his being as water fills a sponge - not dead water a dead sponge - but as a living sap runs through the living sponges of a young oak on the edge of its summer. So that never should he be able to forget it; never henceforth be the same in knowledge or heart or conscience; and nevermore was the lone spiritual battle of his life, if haply waged at all, to be fought out by him with the earlier, simpler weapons of his innocence and his youth, but with all the might of a tempted man's high faith in the beauty and the right and the divine supremacy of goodness.

One morning his wounds had begun to require attention. No one had yet come to him: it was hardly the customary hour: and moreover, by rising in bed he could see that something unusual had drawn the people into the streets. The news of a massacre on the western frontier, perhaps; the arrival of the post-rider with angry despatches from the East; or the torch of revolution thrown far northward from New Orleans. His face had flushed with feverish waiting and he lay with his eyes turned restlessly toward the door.

It was Mrs. Falconer who stepped forward to it with hesitation. But as soon as she caught sight of him, she hurried to the bed. "What is the trouble? Have you been worse?"

"Oh, nothing! It is nothing." "Why do you say that - to me?"

"My shoulder. But it is hardly time for them to come yet." She hesitated and her face showed how serious her struggle was. "Let me," she said firmly.

He looked up quickly, confusedly, at her with a refusal on his lips; but she had already turned away to get the needful things in readiness, and he suffered her, if for no other reason than to avoid letting her see the painful rush of blood to his face. As she moved about the room, she spoke only to ask unavoidable questions; he, only to answer them; and neither looked at the other.

Then he sat up in the bed and bared his neck and

shoulder, one arm and half his chest; and with his face crimson, turned his eyes away. She had been among the women in the fort during that summer thirteen years before, when the battle of the Blue Licks had been fought; and speaking in the quietest, most natural of voices, she now began to describe how the wounded had straggled in from the battle-field; one rifleman reeling on his horse and held in his seat by the arm of a comrade, his bleeding, bandaged head on that comrade's shoulder; another borne on a litter swung between two horses; others - footmen - holding out just long enough to come into sight of the fort, there to sink down; one, a mere youth, fallen a mile back in the hot dusty buffalo trace with an unspoken message to some one in his brave, beautiful, darkening eyes. But before this, she told him how the women had watched all that night and the day previous inside the poor little earth-mound of a defence against artillery, built by order of Jefferson and costing $37.5O; the women taking as always the places of the men who were gone away to the war; becoming as always the defenders of the land, of the children, of those left behind sick or too old to fight. How from the black edge of dawn they had strained their eyes in the direction of the battle until at last a woman's cry of agony had rent the air as the first of the wounded had ridden slowly into sight. How they had rushed forth through the wooden gates and heard the tidings of it all and then had followed the scenes and the things that could never be told for pity and grief and love and sadness.

After a little pause she began to speak of Major Falconer as the school-master had never known her to speak; tremulously of his part in that battle, a Revolutionary officer serving as a common backwoods soldier; eloquently of his perfect courage then and always, of his perfect manliness; and she ended by saying that the worst thing that could ever befall a woman was to marry an unmanly man.

"If any one single thing in life could ever have killed me," she said, "it would have been that."

With her last words she finished the dressing of his wounds. Spots of the deepest rose were on her cheeks; her eyes were lighted with proud fire. Confusedly he thanked her and, lying back on his pillow, closed his eyes and turned his face away.

When she had quickly gone he sat up in the bed again. He drew the book guiltily from under his pillow, looked long and sorrowfully at it, and then with a low cry of shame - the first that had ever burst from his lips - he hurled it across the room and threw himself violently down again, with his forehead against the logs, his eyes hidden, his face burning.

XIV

THE first day that John felt strong enough to walk as far as that end of the town, he was pulling himself unsteadily past the shop when he saw Peter and turned in to rest and chat.The young blacksmith refused to speak to him.

"Peter!" said John with a sad, shaky voice, holding out his hand, "have I changed so much? Don't you know me?"

"Yes; I know you," said Peter. "I wish I didn't."

"I don't think I recognize you any more," replied John, after a moment of silence. "What's the matter?"

"Oh, you get along," said Peter. "Clear out!"

John went inside and drank a gourd of water out of Peter's cool bucket, came back with a stool and sat down squarely before him.

"Now look here," he said with the candour which was always the first law of nature with him, "what have I done to you?"

Peter would neither look nor speak; but being power-less before kindness, he was beginning to break down.

"Out with it," said John. "What have I done?""You know what you've said."

"What have I said about you?" asked John, now perceiving that some mischief had been at work here. "Who told you I had said anything about you?"

"It's no use for you to deny it."

"Who told you?"

"O'Bannon!"

"O'Bannon!" exclaimed John with a frown. "I've never talked to O'Bannon about you - about anything."

"You haven't abused me?" said Peter, wheeling on the schoolmaster, eyes and face and voice full of the suffering of his wounded self-love and of his wounded affection.

"I hope I've abused nobody!" said John proudly.

"Come in here!" cried Peter, springing up and hurrying into his shop.

Near the door stood a walnut tree with wide-spreading branches wearing the fresh plumes of late May, plumes that hung down over the door and across the windows, suffusing the interior with a soft twilight of green and brown shadows. A shaft of sunbeams penetrating a crevice fell on the white neck of a yellow collie that lay on the ground with his head on his paws, his eyes fixed reproachfully on the heels of the horse outside, his ears turned back toward his master. Beside him a box had been kicked over: tools and shoes scattered. A faint line of blue smoke sagged from the dying coals of the forge toward the door, creeping across the anvil bright as if tipped with silver. And in one of the darkest corners of the shop, near a bucket of water in which floated a huge brown gourd, Peter and John sat on a bench while the story of O'Bannon's mischief-making was begun and finished. It was told by Peter with much cordial rubbing of his elbows in the palms of his hands and much light-hearted smoothing of his apron over his knees. At times a cloud, passing beneath the sun, threw the shop into heavier shadow; and then the school-master's dark figure faded into the tone of the sooty wall behind him and only his face, with the contrast of its white linen collar below and the bare discernible lights of his auburn hair above - his face, proud, resolute, astounded, pallid, suffering - started out of the gloom like a portrait from an old canvas.

"And this is why you never came to see me." He had sprung up like a man made well, and was holding Peter's hand and looking reproachfully into his eyes.

"I'd have seen you dead first," cried Peter gaily, giving him a mighty slap on the shoulder. "But wait! O'Bannon's not the only man who can play a joke!"

John hurriedly left the shop with a gesture which Peter did not understand.

The web of deceptive circumstances that had been spun about him had been brushed away at last: he saw the whole truth now - saw his own blindness, blundering, folly, injustice.

He was on his way to Amy already.

When he had started out, he had thought he should walk around a little and then lie down again. Now with his powerful stride come back to him, he had soon passed the last house of the town and was nearing the edge of the wilderness. He took the same straight short course of the afternoon on which he had asked Mrs. Falconer's consent to his suit. As he hurried on, it seemed to him a long time since then! What experiences he had undergone! What had he not suffered! How he was changed!

"Yes," he said over and over to himself, putting away all other thoughts in a resolve to think of this nearest duty only. "If I've been unkind to her, if I've been wrong, have I not suffered?"

He had not gone far before his strength began to fail. He was forced to sit down and rest. It was near sundown when he reached the clearing.

"At last!" he said gratefully, with his old triumphant habit of carrying out whatever he undertook. He had put out all his strength to get there.

He passed the nearest field - the peach trees - the garden - and took the path toward the house.

"Where shall I find her?" he thought. "Where can I see her alone?"

"Between him and the house stood a building of logs and plaster. It was a single room used for the spinning and the weaving of which she had charge. Many a time he had lain on the great oaken chest into which the homespun cloth was stored while she sat by her spinning-wheel; many a talk they had had there together, many a parting; and many a Saturday twilight he had put his arms around her there and turned away for his lonely walk to town, planning their future. "If she should only be in the weaving-room!"

He stepped softly to the door and looked in. She was there - standing near the middle of the room with her face turned from him. The work of the day was done. On one side were the spinning-wheels, farther on a loom; before her a table on which the cloth was piled ready to be folded away; on the other the great open chest into which she was about to store it. She had paused in revery, her hands clasped behind her head.

At the sight of her and with the remembrance of how he had misjudged and mistreated her - most of all swept on by some lingering flood of the old tenderness - he stepped forward put his arms softly around her, drew her closely to him, and buried his check against hers:

"Amy!" he murmured, his voice quivering his whole body trembling, his heart knocking against his ribs like a stone. She struggled out of his arms with a cry and recognizing him, drew her figure up to its full height. Her eyes filled with passion, cold and resentful.

He made a gesture.

"Wait!" he cried. "Listen."

He laid bare everything - from his finding of the bundle to the evening of the ball.

He was standing by the doorway. A small window in the opposite wall of the low room opened toward the

West. Through this a crimson light fell upon his face revealing its pallor, its storm, its struggle for calmness.

She stood a few yards off with her face in shadow. As she had stepped backward, one of her hands had struck against her spinning-wheel and now rested on it; with the other she had caught the edge of the table. From the spinning-wheel a thread of flax trailed to the ground; on the table lay a pair of iron shears.

As he stood looking at her facing him thus in cold half-shadowy anger - at the spinning wheel with its trailing flax - at, the table with its iron shears - at her hands stretched forth as if about to grasp the one and to lay hold on the other - he shudderingly thought of the ancient arbitress of Life and Death - Fate the mighty, the relentless. The fancy passed and was succeeded by the sense of her youth and loveliness. She wore a dress of coarse snow-white homespun, narrow in the skirt and fitting close to her arms and neck and to the outlines of her form. Her hair was parted simply over her low beautiful brow. There was nowhere a ribbon or a trifle of adornment: and in that primitive, simple, fearless revelation of itself her figure had the frankness of a statue. While he spoke the anger died out of her face. But in its stead came something worse - hardness; and something that was worse still - an expression of revenge.

"If I was unfeeling with you," he implored, "only consider! You had broken your engagement without giving any reason; I saw you at the party dancing with Joseph; I believed myself trifled with, I said that if you could treat in that way there was nothing you could say that I cared to hear. I was blind to the truth; I was blinded by suffering.

"If you suffered, it was your own fault," she replied, calm as the Fate that holds the shears and the thread. "I wanted to explain to you why I broke my engagement and why I went with Joseph: you refused to allow me."

"But before that! Remember that I had gone to see you the night before. You had a chance to explain then. But you did not explain. Still, I did not doubt that your reason was good. I did not ask you to state it. But when I saw you at the party with Joseph, was I not right, in thinking that the time for an explanation had passed?"

"No," she replied. "As long as I did not give any reason, you ought not to have asked for one; but when I wished to give it, you should have been ready to hear it." He drew himself up quickly.

"This is a poor pitiful misunderstanding. I say, forgive me! We will let it pass. I had thought each of us was wrong - you first, I, afterward." "I was not wrong either first or last!"

"Think so if you must! Only, try to understand me! Amy, you know I've loved you. You could never have acted toward me as you have, if you had not believed that. And that night - the night you would not see me alone - I went to ask you to marry me. I meant to ask you the next night. I am here to ask you now! . . ."

He told her of the necessity that had kept him from speaking sooner, of the recent change which made it possible. He explained how he had waited and planned and had shaped his whole life with the thought that she would share it. She had listened with greater interest especially to what he had said about the improvement in his fortunes. Her head had dropped slightly forward as though she were thinking that after all perhaps she had made a mistake. But she now lifted it with deliberateness:

"And what right had you to be so sure all this time that I would marry you whenever you asked me? What right had you to take it for granted that whenever you were ready, I would be?"

The hot flush of shame dyed his face that she could deal herself such a wound and not even know it.

He drew himself up again, sparing her:

"I loved you. I could not love without hoping. I could not hope without planning. Hoping, planning, striving, - everything! - it was all because I loved you!" And then he waited, looking down on her in silence.

She began to grow nervous. She had stooped to pick up the thread of flax and was passing it slowly between her fingers. When he spoke again, his voice showed that he shook like a man with a chill: "I have said all I can say. I have offered all I have to offer. I am waiting."

Still the silence lasted for the new awe of him that began to fall upon her. In ways she could not fathom she was beginning to feel that a change had come over him during these weeks of their separation. He used more gentleness with her: his voice, his manner, his whole bearing, had finer courtesy; he had strangely ascended to some higher level of character, and he spoke to her from this distance with a sadness that touched her indefinably - with a larger manliness that had its quick effect. She covertly lifted her eyes and beheld on his face a proud passion of beauty and of pain beyond anything that she had ever thought possible to him or to any man. She quickly dropped her head again; she shifted her position; a band seemed to tighten around her throat; until, in a voice hardly to be heard, she murmured falteringly:

"I have promised to marry Joseph."

He did not speak or move, but continued to stand leaning against the lintel of the doorway, looking down on her. The colour was fading from the west leaving it ashen white. And so standing in the dying radiance, he saw the long bright day of his young hope come to its close; he drained to its dregs his cup of bitterness she had prepared for him; learned his first lesson in the victory of little things over the larger purposes of life, over the nobler planning; bit the dust of the heart's first defeat and tragedy.

She had caught up the iron shears in her nervousness and begun to cut the flaxen thread; and in the silence of the room only the rusty click was now heard as she clipped it, clipped it, clipped it.

Then such a greater trembling seized her that she laid the shears back upon the table. Still he did not move or speak, and there seemed to fall upon her conscience - in insupportable burden until, as if by no will of her own, she spoke again pitifully:

"I didn't know that you cared so much for me. It isn't my fault. You had never asked me, and he had already asked me twice." He changed his position quickly so that the last light coming in through the window could no longer betray his face. All at once his voice broke

James Lane Allen

through the darkness, so unlike itself that she started:

"When did you give him this promise? I have no right to ask . . . when did you give him this promise?"

She answered as if by no will of her own:"The night of the ball - as we were going home."

She waited until she felt that she should sink to the ground.

Then he spoke again as if rather to himself than to her, and with the deepest sorrow and pity for them both:

"If I had gone with you that night - if I had gone with you that night - and had asked you - you would have married me."

Her lips began to quiver and all that was in her to break down before him - to yearn for him. In a voice neither could scarce hear she said:

"I will marry you yet!"

She listened. She waited, Out of the darkness she could distinguish not the rustle of a movement, not a breath of sound; and at last cowering back into herself with shame, she buried her face in her hands.

Then she was aware that he had come forward and was standing over her. He bent his head down so close that his lids touched her hair - so close that his warm breath was on her forehead - and she felt rather than knew him saying to himself, not to her:

"Good-bye!"

He passed like a tall spirit out of the door, and she heard his footsteps die away along the path - die slowly away as of one who goes never to return.

XV

A JEST may be the smallest pebble that was ever dropped into the sunny mid-ocean of the mind; but sooner or later it sinks to a hard bottom, sooner or later sends it ripples toward the shores where the caves of the fatal passions yawn and roar for wreckage. It is the Comedy of speech that forever dwells as Tragedy's fondest sister, sharing with her the same unmarked domain; for the two are but identical forces of the mind in gentle and in ungentle action as one atmosphere holds within itself unseparated the zephyr and the storm.

The following afternoon O'Bannon was ambling back to town - slowly and awkwardly, he being a poor rider and dreading a horse's back as he would have avoided its kick. He was returning from the paper mill at Georgetown whither he had been sent by Mr. Bradford with an order for a further supply of sheets. The errand had not been a congenial one; and he was thinking now as often before that he would welcome any chance of leaving the editor's service. What he had always coveted since his coming into the wilderness was the young master's school; for the Irish teacher, afterwards so well known a figure in the West, was even at this time beginning to bend his mercurial steps across the mountains. Out of his covetousness had sprung perhaps his enmity toward the master, whom he further despised for his Scotch blood, and in time had grown to dislike from motives of jealousy, and last of all to hate for his simple purity. Many a man nurses a grudge of this kind against his human brother and will take pains to punish him accordingly; for success in virtue is as hard for certain natures to witness as success in anything else will irritate those whose nerveless or impatient or ill-directed grasp it has wisely eluded.

On all accounts therefore it had fallen well to his purpose to make the schoolmaster the dupe of a disagreeable jest. The jest had had unexpectedly serious consequences: it had brought about the complete discomfiture of John in his love affair; it had caused the trouble behind the troubled face with which he had looked out upon every one during his illness.

The two young men had never met since; but the one was under a cloud; the other was refulgent with his petty triumph; and he had set his face all the more toward any further aggressiveness that occasion should bring happily to his hand.

The mere road might have shamed him into manlier reflections. It was one of the forest highways of the majestic bison opened ages before into what must have been to them Nature's most gorgeous kingdom, her fairest, most magical Babylon: with hanging gardens of verdure everywhere swung from the tree-domes to the ground; with the earth one vast rolling garden of softest verdure and crystal waters: an ancient Babylon of the Western woods, most alluring and in the end most fatal to the luxurious, wantoning wild creatures, which know no sin and are never found wanting.

This old forest street of theirs, so broad, so roomy, so

arched with hoary trees, so silent now and filled with the pity and pathos of their ruin - it may not after all have been marked out by them. But ages before they had ever led their sluggish armies eastward to the Mississippi and, crossing, had shaken its bright drops from their shaggy low-hung necks on the eastern bank - ages before this, while the sun of human history was yet silvering the dawn of the world - before Job's sheep lay sick in the land of Uz - before a lion had lain down to dream in the jungle where Babylon was to arise and to become a name, - this old, old, old high road may have been a footpath of the awful mastodon, who had torn his terrible way through the tangled, twisted, gnarled and rooted fastnesses of the wilderness as lightly as a wild young Cyclone out of the South tears his way through the ribboned corn.

Ay, for ages the mastodon had trodden this dust. And, ay, for ages later the bison. And, ay, for ages a people, over whose vanished towns and forts and graves had grown the trees of a thousand years, holding in the mighty claws of their roots the dust of those long, long secrets. And for centuries later still along this path had crept or rushed or fled the Indians: now coming from over the moon-loved, fragrant, passionate Southern mountains; now from the sad frozen forests and steely marges of the Lakes: both eager for the chase. For into this high road of the mastodon and the bison smaller pathways entered from each side, as lesser water-courses run into a river: the avenues of the round-horned elk, narrow, yet broad enough for the tossing of his lordly antlers; the trails of the countless migrating shuffling bear; the slender woodland alleys along which buck and doe and fawn had sought the springs or crept tenderly from their breeding coverts or fled like shadows in the race for life; the devious wolf-runs of the maddened packs as they had sprung to the kill; the threadlike passages of the stealthy fox; the tiny trickle of the squirrel, crossing, recrossing, without number; and ever close beside all these, unseen, the grass-path or the tree-path of the cougar. Ay, both eager for the chase at first and then more eager for each other's death for the sake of the whole chase: so that this immemorial game-trace had become a war-path - a long dim forest street alive with the advance and retreat of plume-bearing, vermilion-painted armies; and its rich black dust, on which hereand there a few scars of sunlight now lay like stillest thinnest yellow leaves, had been dyed from end to end with the red of the heart.

And last of all into this ancient woodland street of war one day there had stepped a strange new-comer - the Anglo-Saxon. Fairhaired, blue-eyed, always a lover of Land and of Woman and therefore of Home; in whose blood beat the conquest of many a wilderness before this - the wilderness of Britain, the wilderness of Normandy, the wildernesses of the Black, of the Hercinian forest, the wilderness of the frosted marshes of the Elbe and the Rhine and of the North Sea's wildest wandering foam and fury.

Here white lover and red lover had metand fought: with the same high spirit and overstrung will, scorn of danger, greed of pain; the same vehemence of hatred and excess of revenge; the same ideal of a hero as a young man who stands in the thick of carnage calm and unconscious of his wounds or rushes gladly to any poetic beauty of death that is terrible and sublime. And already the red lover was gone and the fair-haired lover stood the quiet owner of the road, the last of all its long train of conquerors brute and human - with his cabin near by, his wife smiling beside the spinning-wheel, his baby crowing on the threshold. History was thicker here than along the Appian Way and it might well have stirred O'Bannon; but he rode shamblingly on, untouched, unmindful. At every bend his eye quickly swept along the stretch of road to the next turn; for every man carried the eye of an eagle in his head in those days.

At one point he pulled his horse up violently. A large buckeye tree stood on the roadside a hundred yards ahead. Its large thick leaves already full at this season, drew around the trunk a seamless robe of darkest green. But a single slight rent had been made on one side as though a bough bad been lately broken off to form an aperture commanding a view of the road; and through this aperture he could see something black within-as black as a crow's wing.

O'Bannon sent his horse forward in the slowest walk: it was unshod; the stroke of its hoofs was muffled by the dust; and he had approached quite close, remaining himself unobserved, before he recognized the schoolmaster.

He was reclining against the trunk, his hat off, his eyes closed; in the heavy shadows he looked white and sick and weak and troubled. Plainly he was buried deep in his own thoughts. If he had broken off those low boughs in order that he might obtain a view of the road, he had forgotten his own purpose; if he had walked all the way out to this spot and was waiting, his vigilance had grown lax, his aim slipped from him.

Perhaps before his eyes the historic vision of the road had risen: that crowded pageant, brute and human, all whose red passions, burning rights and burning wrongs, frenzied fightings and awful deaths had left but the sun-scarred dust, the silence of the woods clothing itself in green. And from this panoramic survey it may have come to him to feel the shortness of the day of his own life, the pitifulness of its earthly contentions, and above everything else the sadness of the necessity laid upon him to come down to the level of the cougar and the wolf.

But as O'Bannon struck his horse and would have passed on, he sprang up quickly enough and walked out into the middle of the road. When the horse's head was near he quietly took hold of the reins and throwing his weight slightly forward, brought it to a stop.

"Let go!" exclaimed O'Bannon, furious and threatening.

He did let go, and stepping backward three paces, he threw off his coat and waistcoat and tossed them aside to the green bushes: the action was a pathetic mark of his lifelong habit of economy in clothes: a coat must under all circumstances be cared for. He tore off his neckcloth so that his high shirt collar fell away from his neck, showing the purple scar of his wound; and he girt his trousers in about his waist, as a laboring man will trim himself for neat, quick, violent work. Then with a long stride he came round to the side of the horse's head, laid his hand on its neck and looked O'Bannon in the eyes:

"At first I thought I'd wait till you got back to town. I wanted to catch you on the street or, in a tavern where others could witness. I'm sorry. I'm ashamed I ever wished any man to see me lay my hand on you.

"Since you came out to Kentucky, have I ever crossed you? Thwarted you in any plan or purpose? Wronged you in any act? Ill-used your name? By anything I have thought or wished or done taken from the success of your life or made success harder for you to win?

"But you had hardly come out here before you began to attack me and you have never stopped. Out of all this earth's prosperity you have envied me my little share: you have tried to take away my school. With your own good name gone, you have wished to befoul mine. With no force of character to rise in the world, you have sought to drag me down. When I have avoided a brawl with you, preferring to live my life in peace with every man, you have said I was a coward, you unmanly slanderer! When I have desired to live the best life I could, you have turned even that against me. You lied and you know you lied - blackguard! You have laughed at the blood in my veins - the sacred blood of my mother - "

His words choked him. The Scotch blood, so slow to kindle like a mass of cold anthracite, so terrible with heat to the last ashes, was burning in him now with flameless fury.

"I passed it all over, I only asked to go on my way and have you go yours. But now - " He seemed to realize in an instant everything that he had suffered in consequence of O'Bannon's last interference in his affairs. He ground his teeth together and shook his head from side to side like an animal that had seized its prey.

"Get down!" he cried, throwing his head back. "I can't fight you as an equal but I will give you one beating for the low dog you are."

O'Bannon had listened immovable. He now threw the reins down and started to throw his leg over the saddle but resumed his seat. "Let go!" he shouted. "I will not be held and ordered."

The school-master tightened his grasp on the reins. "Get down! I don't trust you."

O'Bannon held a short heavy whip. He threw this into the air and caught it by the little end.

The school-teacher sprang to seize it; but O'Bannon lifted it backward over his shoulder, and then raising himself high in his stirrups, brought it down. The master saw it coming and swerved so that it grazed his ear; but it cut into the wound on his neck with a coarse, ugly, terrific blow and the blood spurted. With a loud cry of agony and horror, he reeled and fell backward dizzy and sick and nigh to fainting. The next moment in the deadly silence of a wild beast attacking to kill, he was on his feet, seized the whip before it could fall again, flung it away, caught O'Bannon's arm and planting his foot against the horse's shoulder, threw his whole weight backward. The saddle turned, the horse sprang aside, and he fell again, pulling O'Bannon heavily down on him.

There in the blood-dyed dust of the old woodland street, where bison and elk, stag and lynx, wolf and cougar and bear had gored or torn each other during the centuries before; there on the same level, glutting their passion, their hatred, their revenge, the men fought out their strength - the strength of that King of Beasts whose den is where it should be: in a man's spirit.

A few afternoons after this a group of rough young fellows were gathered at Peter's shop. The talk had turned to the subject of the fight: and every one had thrown his gibe at O'Bannon, who had taken it with equal good nature. From this they had chaffed him on his fondness for a practical joke and his awkward riding; and out of this, he now being angry, grew a bet with Horatio Turpin that he could ride the latter's filly, standing hitched to the fence of the shop. He was to ride it three times around the enclosure, and touch it once each time in the flank with the spur which the young horseman took from his heel.

At the first prick of it, the high-spirited mettlesome animal, scarcely broken, reared and sprang forward, all but unseating him. He dropped the reins and instincttively caught its mane, at the same time pressing his legs more closely in against the animal's sides, thus driving the spur deeper. They shouted to him to lie down, to fall off, as they saw the awful danger ahead; for the maddened filly, having run wildly around the enclosure several times, turned and rushed straight toward the low open doors of the smithy and the pasture beyond. But he would not release his clutch; and with his body bent a little forward, he received the blow of the projecting shingles full on his head as the mare shot from under him into the shop, scraping him off.

They ran to him and lifted him out of the sooty dust and laid him on the soft green grass. But of consciousness there was never to be more for him: his jest had reached its end.

IT was early summer now. In the depths of the greening woods the school-master lay reading:

"And thus it passed on from Candlemass until after Easter that the month of May was come, when every lusty heart beginneth to blossom and to bring forth fruit; for like as herbs and trees bring forth fruit and flourish in May, in likewise, every lusty heart that is any manner a lover springeth and flourisheth in lusty deeds. For it giveth unto all lovers courage - that lusty month of May - in something to constrain him to some manner of thing more in that month than in any other month. For diverse causes: For then all herbs and trees renew a man and woman; and, in likewise, lovers call again to their mind old gentleness and old service and many kind deeds that were forgotten by negligence. For like as winter rasure doth always erase and deface green summer, so fareth it by unstable love in man and woman. For in many persons there is no stability;...for a little blast of winter's rasure, anon we shall deface and lay apart true love (for little or naught), that cost so much. This is no wisdom nor stability, but it is feebleness of nature and great disworship whomever useth this. Therefore like as May month flowereth and flourisheth in many gardens, so in likewise let every man of worship flourish his heart in this world: first unto God, and next unto the joy of them that he promised his faith unto; for there was never worshipful man nor worshipful woman but they loved one better than the other. And worship in arms may never be foiled; but first reserve the honour to God, and secondly the quarrel must come of thy lady; and such love I call virtuous love. But nowsdays men cannot love seven nights but they must have all their desires... Right so fareth love nowadays, soon hot, soon cold: this is no stability. But the old love was not so. Men and women could love together seven years...and then was love truth and faithfulness. And lo! In likewise was used love in King Arthur's days. Wherefore I liken love nowadays unto summer and winter; for like the one is hot and the other cold, so fareth love nowadays."......

He laid the book aside upon the grass, sat up, and mournfully looked about him. Effort was usually needed to withdraw his mind from those low-down shadowy centuries over into which of late by means of the book, as by means of a bridge spanning a known and an unknown land, he had crossed, and wonder-stricken had wandered; but these words brought him swiftly home to the country of his own sorrow. Unstable love! feebleness of nature! one blast of a cutting winter wind and lo! green summer defaced: the very phrases seemed shaped by living lips close to the ear of his experience. It was in this spot a few weeks ago that he had planned his future with Amy: these were the acres he would buy; on this hill-top he would build; here, home-sheltered, wife-anchored, the warfare of his flesh and spirit ended, he could begin to put forth all his strength upon the living of his life. Had any frost ever killed the bud of nature's hope more unexpectedly than this landscape now lay blackened before him? And had any summer ever cost so much?

What could strike a man as a more mortal wound than to lose the woman he had loved and in losing her see her lose her loveliness? As the end of it all, he now found himself sitting on the blasted rock of his dreams in the depths of the greening woods. He was well again by this time and conscious of that retightened grasp upon health and redder stir of life with which the great Mother-nurse, if she but dearly love a man, will tend him and mend him and set him on his feet again from a bed of wounds or sickness. It had happened to him also that with this reflushing of his blood there had reached him the voice of Summer advancing northward to all things and making all things common in their awakening and their aim.

He knew of old the pipe of this imperious Shepherd; sounding along the inner vales of his being; herding him toward universal fellowship with seeding grass and breeding herb and every heart-holding creature of the woods. He perfectly recognized the sway of the thrilling pipe; he perfectly realized the joy of the jubilant fellowship. And it was with eyes the more mournful therefore that he gazed in purity about him at the universal miracle of old life passing into new life, at the divinely appointed and divinely fulfilled succession of forms, at the unrent mantle of the generations being visibly woven around him under the golden goads of the sun. " ...for like as herbs bring forth fruit and flourish in May, in likewise, every heart that is in any manner a lover spingeth and flourisheth in lusty deeds." . . . But all this must come, must spend itself, must pass him by, as a flaming pageant dies away from a beholder who is forbidden to kindle his own torch and claim his share of its innocent revels. He too had laid his plans to celebrate his marriage at the full tide of the Earth's joy, and these plans had

James Lane Allen

failed him.

But while the school-master thus was gloomily contemplating the end of his relationship with Amy and her final removal from the future of his life, in reality another and larger trouble was looming close ahead. A second landscape had begun to beckon not like his poor little frost-killed field, not of the earth at all, but lifted unattainable into the air, faint, clear, elusive - the marriage of another woman. And how different she! He felt sure that no winter's rasure would ever reach that land; no instability, no feebleness of nature awaited him there; the loveliness of its summer, now brooding at flood, would brood unharmed upon it to the natural end.

He buried his face guiltily in his hands as he tried to shut out the remembrance of how persistently of late, whithersoever he had turned, this second image had reappeared before him, growing always clearer, drawing always nearer, summoning him more luringly. Already he had begun to know the sensations of a traveller who is crossing sands with a parched tongue and a weary foot, crossing toward a country that he will never reach, but that he will stagger toward as long as he has strength to stand. During the past several days - following his last interview with Amy - he had realized for the first time how long and how plainly the figure of Mrs. Falconer had been standing before him and upon how much loftier a level. Many a time of old, while visiting the house, he had grown tired of Amy; but he had never felt wearied by her. For Amy he was always making apologies to his own conscience; she needed none. He had secretly hoped that in time Amy would become more what he wished his wife to be; it would have pained him to think of her as altered. Often he had left Amy's company with a grateful sense of regaining the larger liberty of his own mind; by her he always felt guided to his better self, he carried away her ideas with the hope of making them his ideas, he was set on fire with a spiritual passion to do his utmost in the higher strife of the world.

For this he had long paid her the guiltless tribute of his reverence and affection. And between his reverence and affection and all the forbidden that lay beyond rose a barrier which not even his imagination had ever consciously overleaped. Now the forbidding barrier had disappeared, and in its place had appeared the forbidden bond - he knew not how or when. How could he? Love, the Scarlet Spider, will in a night hang between two that have been apart a web too fine for either to see; but the strength of both will never avail to break it.

Very curiously it had befallen him furthermore that just at the time when all these changes were taking place around him and within him, she had brought him the book that she had pressed with emphasis upon his attention. In the backwoods settlements of Pennsylvania where his maternal Scotch-Irish ancestors had settled and his own life been spent, very few volumes had fallen into his hands. After coming to Kentucky not many more until of late: so that of the world's history he was still a stinted and hungry student. When,therefore, she had given him Malory's "LeMorte D'Arthur," it was the first time that the ideals of chivalry had ever flashed their glorious light upon him; for the first time the models of Christian manhood, on which western Europe nourished itself for centuries, displayed themselves to his imagination with the charm of story; he heard of Camelot, of the king, of that company of men who strove with each other in arms, but strove also with each other in grace of life and for the immortal mysteries of the spirit. She had said that he should have read this book long before but that henceforth he would always need it even more than in his past: that here were some things he had looked for in the world and had never found; characters such as he had always wished to grapple to himself as his abiding comrades: that if he would love the best that it loved, hate what it hated, scorn what it scorned, it would help him in the pursuit of his own ideals to the end. Of this and more he felt at once the truth, since of all earthly books known to him this contained the most heavenly revelation of what a man may be in manliness, in gentleness, and in goodness. And as he read the nobler portions of the book, the nobler parts of his nature gave out their immediate response. Hungrily he hurried to and fro across the harvest of those fertile pages, gathering of the white wheat of the spirit many a lustrous sheaf: the love of courage, the love of courtesy, the love of honour, the love of high aims and great actions, the love of the poor and the helpless, the love of a spotless name and a spotless life, the love of kindred, the love of friendship, the love of humility of spirit, the love of forgiveness, the love of beauty, the love of love, the love of God. Surely, he said to himself, within the band of these virtues lay not only a man's noblest life, but the noblest life of the world.

While fondling these, he failed not to notice how the great book, as though it were a living mouth, spat its deathless scorn upon the things that he also - in the imperfect measure of his powers - had always hated: all cowardice of mind or body, all lying, all oppression, all unfaithfulness, all secret revenge and hypocrisy and double-dealing: the smut of the heart and mind. But ah! the other things besides these.

Sown among the white wheat of the spirit were the red tares of the flesh; and as he strode back and forth through the harvest, he found himself plucking these also with feverish vehemence. There were things here that he had never seen in print: words that he had never even named to his secret consciousness; thoughts and desires that he had put away from his soul with many a struggle, many a prayer; stories of a kind that he had always declined to hear when told in companies of men: all here, spelled out, barefaced, without apology, without shame: the deposits of those old, old moral voices and standards long since buried deep under the ever rising level of the world's whitening holiness. With utter guilt and shame he did not leave off till he had plucked the last red tare; and having plucked them, he had hugged the whole inflaming bundle against his blood - his blood now flushed with youth, flushed with health, flushed with summer.

And finally, in the midst of all these things, perhaps coloured by them, there had come to him the first great awakening of his life in a love that was forbidden.

He upbraided himself the more bitterly for the influence of the book because it was she who had placed both the good and the evil in his hand with perfect confidence that he would lay hold on the one and remain unsoiled by the other. She had remained spirit-proof herself against the influences that tormented him; out of her own purity she had judged him. And yet, on the other hand, with that terrible candour of mind which he used either for or against himself as rigidly as for or against another person, he

James Lane Allen

pleaded in his own behalf that she had made a mistake in overestimating his strength, in underestimating his temptations. How should she know that for years his warfare had gone on direfully? How realize that almost daily he had stood as at the dividing of two roads: the hard, narrow path ascending to the bleak white peaks of the spirit; the broad, sweet, downward vistas of the flesh? How foresee, therefore, that the book would only help to rend him in twain with a mightier passion for each?

He had been back at the school a week now. He had never dared go to see her. Confront that luminous face with his darkened one? Deal such a soul the wound of such dishonour? He knew very well that the slightest word or glance of self-betrayal would bring on the immediate severance of her relationship with him: her wifehood might be her martyrdom, but it was martyrdom inviolate. And yet he felt that if he were once with her, he could not be responsible for the consequences: he could foresee no degree of self-control that would keep him from telling her that he loved her. He had been afraid to go. But ah, how her image drew him day and night, day and night! Slipping between him and every other being, every other desire. Her voice kept calling to him to come to her - a voice new, irresistible, that seemed to issue from the deeps of Summer, from the deeps of Life, from the deeps of Love, with its almighty justification.

This was his first Saturday. To-day he had not even the school as a post of duty, to which he might lash himself for safety. He had gone away from town in an opposite direction from her home, burying himself alone in the forest. But between him and that summoning voice he could put no distance. It sang out afresh to him from the inviting silence of the woods as well as from its innumerable voices. It sang to him reproachfully from the pages of the old book: "In the lusty month of May lovers call again to their mind old gentleness and old service and many deeds that were forgotten by negligence:" he had never even gone to thank her for all her kindness to him during his illness!

Still he held out, wrestling with himself. At last Love itself, the deceiver, snaringly pleaded that she alone could cure him of all this folly. It had grown up wholly during his absence from her, no doubt by reason of this. Many a time before be had gone to her about other troubles, and always he had found her carrying that steady light of right-mindedness which had scatteredhis darkness and revealed his better pathway.

He sprang up and set off sternly through the woods. Goaded by love, he fancied that the presence of the forbidden woman would restore him to his old, blameless friendship.

XVIII

SHE was at work in the garden: he had long ago noted that she never idled.

He approached the fence and leaned on it as when they had last talked together; but his big Jacobin hat was pulled down over his eyes now. He was afraid of his own voice, afraid of the sound of his knuckles, so that when at last he had rapped on the fence, he hoped that she had not heard, so that he could go away.

"Knock louder," she called out from under her bonnet. "I'm not sure that I heard you."

How sunny her voice was, how pure and sweet and remote from any suspicion of hovering harm! It unshackled him as from a dreadful nightmare.

He broke into his old laugh - the first time since he had stood there before - and frankly took off his hat.

"How did you know who it was? You saw me coming!"

"Did I? I don't like to contradict a stranger."

"Am I a stranger?"

"What makes a stranger? How long has it been since you were here?"

"A lifetime," he replied gravely. "You are still living! Will you walk into my parlour?"

"Will you meet me at the door?" It was so pleasant to seem gay, to say nothing, be nothing! She came quietly over to the fence and gave him her hand with a little laugh." "You have holiday of Saturdays. I have not, you see. But I can take a recess: come in. You are looking well! Wounds agree with you."

He went trembling round to the gate, passed in, and they sat down on the bench.

"How things grow in this soil," she said pointing to the garden. "It has only been five or six weeks since you were here. Do you remember? I was planting the seed: now look at the plants!"

"I, too, was sowing that afternoon," he replied musingly. "But my harvest ripened before yours; I have already reaped it."

"What's that you are saying about me?" called out a hard, smooth voice from over the fence at their back. "I don't like to miss anything!"

Amy had a piece of sewing, which she proceeded to spread upon the fence.

"Will you show me about this, Aunt Jessica?"

She greeted John without embarrassment or discernible remembrance of their last meeting. Her fine blond hair was frowsy and a button was missing at the throat of her dress. (Some women begin to let themselves go after marriage; some after the promise of marriage.) There were cake-crumbs also in one corner of her mouth. "These are some of my wedding clothes," she said to him prettily. "Aren't they fine?"

Mrs. Falconer drew her attention for a moment and they began to measure the cloth over the back of her finger, counting the lengths under her breath.

Amy took a pin from the bosom of her dress and picked between her pearly teeth daintily.

"Aunt Jessica," she suddenly inquired with mischievous look at John, "before you were engaged to uncle, was there any one else you liked better?"

With a terrible inward start, he shot a covert glance at her and dropped his eyes. Mrs. Falconer's answer was playful and serene.

"It has been a long time; it's hard to remember. But I've heard of such cases."

There was something in the reply that surprised Amy and she peeped under Mrs. Falconer's bonnet to see what was going on. She had learned that a great deal went on under that bonnet. "Well, after you were engaged to him, was there anybody else?"

"I don't think I remember. But I've known of such cases."

Amy peeped again, and the better to see for herself hereafter, coolly lifted the bonnet off. "Well, after you were married to him," she said, "was there anybody else? I've known of such cases," she added, with a dry imitation of the phrase.

"You have made me forget my lengths," said Mrs. Falconer with unruffled innocence. "I'll have to measure again." Amy turned to John with sparkling eyes. "Did you ever know a man who was in love with a married woman?"

"Yes," said John, secretly writhing, but too truthful to say "no."

"What did he do about it?" asked Amy.

"I don't know," replied John, shortly. "What do you think he ought to have done? What would you do?" asked Amy. "I don't know," replied John, more coolly, turning away his confused face.

Neither of you seems to know anything this afternoon," observed Amy, "and I'd always been led to suppose that each of you knew everything."

As she departed with her sewing, she turned to send a final arrow, with some genuine feeling. "I think I'll send for uncle to come and talk tome."

"Stay and talk to us," Mrs. Falconer called to her with a sincere, pitying laugh. "Come back!"

Amy's questions had passed high over her head like a little flock of chattering birds they had struck him low, like bullets.

" Go on , " she said quietly, when they were seated

again, "what was it about the harvest?"

He could not reply at once; and she let him sit in silence, looking across the garden while she took up her knitting from the end of the bench, and leaning lightly toward him, measured a few rows of stitches across his wrist. It gave way under her touch.

"These are your mittens for next winter," she said softly, more softly than he had ever heard her speak. And the quieting melody of her mere tone! - how unlike that other voice which bored joyously into you as a bright gimlet twists its unfeeling head into wood. He turned on her one quick, beautiful look of gratitude.

"What was it about the harvest?" she repeated, forbearing to return his look, and thinking that all his embarrassment followed from the pain of having thus met Amy.

He began to speak very slowly: "The last time I was here I boasted that I had yet to meet my first great defeat in life . . . that there was nothing stronger in the world than a man's will and purpose . . . that if ideals got shattered, we shattered them . . . that I would go on doing with my life as I had planned, be what I wished, have what I wanted."

"Well?" she urged, busy with her needles.

"I know better now."

"Aren't you the better for knowing better?" He made no reply; so that she began to say very simply and as a matter of course: "It's the defeat more than anything else that hurts you! Defeat is always the hardest thing for you to stand, even in trifles. But don't you know that we have to be defeated in order to succeed? Most of us spend half our lives in fighting for things that would only destroy us if we got them. A man who has never been defeated is usually a man who has been ruined. And, of course," she added with light raillery, "of course there are things stronger than the strongest will and purpose: the sum of other men's wills and purposes, for instance. A single soldier may have all the will and purpose to whip an army, but he doesn't do it. And a man may have all the will and purpose to whip the world, walk over it rough-shod, shoulder it out of his way as you'd like to do, but he doesn't do it. And of course we do not shatter our ideals ourselves - always: a thousand things outside ourselves do that for us. And what reason had you to say that you would have what you wanted? Your wishes are not infallible. Suppose you craved the forbidden?"

She looked over at him archly, but he jerked his face farther away. Then he spoke out with the impulse to get away from her question:

"I could stand to be worsted by great things. But the little ones, the low, the coarse, the trivial! Ever since I was here last - beginning that very night - I have been struggling like a beast with his foot in a trap. I don't mean Amy!" he cried apologetically.

"I'm glad you've discovered there are little things," she replied. "I had feared you might never find that out. I'm not sure yet that you have. One of your great troubles is that everything in life looks too large to you, too serious, too important. You fight the gnats of the world as you fought your panther. With you everything is a mortal combat. You run every butterfly down and break it on an iron wheel; after you have broken it, it doesn't matter: everything is as it was before, except that you have lost time and strength. The only things that need trouble us very much are not the things it is right to conquer, but the things it is wrong to conquer. If you ever conquer in yourself anything that is right, that will be a real trouble for you as long as you live - and for me!"

He turned quickly and sat facing her, the muscles of his face moving convulsively. She did not look at him, but went on:

"The last time you were here, you told me that I did not appreciate Amy; that I could not do her justice; but that no woman could ever understand why a man loved any other woman."

"Did I say that?" he muttered remorsefully.

"It was because you did not appreciate he - it was because you would never be able to do her justice - that I was so opposed to the marriage. And this was largely a question of little things. I knew perfectly well that as soon as you married Amy, you would begin to expect her to act as though she were made of iron: so many pieces, so many wheels, so many cogs, so many revolutions. All the inevitable little things that make up the most of her life - that make up so large a part of every woman's life - the little moods, the little play, little changes, little tempers and inconsistencies and contradictions and falsities and hypocrisies which come every morning and go every night, - all these would soon have been to you - oh! I'm afraid they'd have been as big as a herd of buffalo! There would have been a bull fight for every foible."

She laughed out merrily, but she did not look at him.

"Yes," she continued, trying to drain his cup for him, since he would not do it himself, "you are the last man in the world to do a woman like Amy justice. I'm afraid you will never do justice to any woman, unless you change a good deal and learn a good deal. Perhaps no woman will ever understand you - except me."

She looked up at him now with the clearest fondness in her exquisite eyes.

With a groan he suddenly leaned over and buried his face in his hands. His hat fell over on the grass. Her knitting dropped to her lap, and one of her hands went out quickly toward his big head, heavy with its shaggy reddish mass of hair, which had grown long during his sickness. But at the first touch she quickly withdrew it, and stooping over picked up his hat and put it on her knees, and sat beside him silent and motionless.

He straightened himself up a moment later, and keeping his face turned away reached for his hat and drew it down over his eyes.

"I can't tell you! You don't understand!" he said in a broken voice.

"I understand everything. Amy has told me-poor little Amy! She is not wholly to blame. I blame you more. You may have been in love with your idea of her, but anything like that idea she never has been and never will be; and who is responsible for your idea, then, but yourself? It is a mistake that many a man makes; and when the woman disappoints him, he blames her, and deserts her or makes her life a torment. Of course a woman may make the same mistake; but, as a rule, women are better judges of men than men are of women. Besides, if they find themselves mistaken, they bear their disappointment better and show it less: they alone know their tragedy; it is the unperceived that kills."

The first tears that he had ever seen gathered and dimmed her eyes. She was too proud either to acknowledge them or to hide them. Her lids fell quickly to curtain them in, and the lashes received them in their long, thick fringes. But she had suffered herself to go too far.

"Ah, if you had loved her! loved her!" she cried with an intensity of passion, a weary, immeasurable yearning, that seemed to come from a life in death. The strength of that cry struck him as a rushing wind strikes a young eagle on the breast, lifting him from his rock and setting him afloat on the billows of a rising storm. His spirit mounted the spirit of her unmated confession, rode it as its master, exulted in it as his element and his home. But the stricken man remained motionless on the bench a few feet from the woman, looking straight across the garden, with his hands clinched about his knees, his hat hiding his eyes, his jaws set sternly with the last grip of resolution.

It was some time before either spoke. Then her voice was very quiet.

"You found out your mistake in time; suppose it had been too late? But this is all so sad; we will never speak of it again. Only you ought to feel that from this time you can go on with the plans of your life uninterrupted. Begin with all this as small defeat that means a larger victory! There is no entanglement now, not a drawback; what a future! It does look as though you might now have everything that you set your heart on."

She glanced up at him with a mournful smile, and taking the knitting which had lain forgotten in her lap leaned over again and measured the stitches upon his wrist.

"When do you start?" she asked, seeing a terrible trouble gathering in his face and resolved to draw his thoughts to other things.

"Next week."

The knitting fell again.

"And you have allowed all this time to go by without coming to see us! You are to come everyday till you go: promise!"

He had been repeating that he would not trust himself to come at all again, except to say good-bye.

"I can't promise that."

"But we want you so much! The major wants you, I want you more than the major. Why should meeting Amy be so hard? Remember how long it will be before you get back. When will you be back?"

He was thinking it were better never.

"It is uncertain," he said.

"I shall begin to look for you as soon as you are gone. I can hear your horse's feet now, rustling in the leaves of October. But what will become of me till then? Ah, you don't begin to realize how much you are to me!"

"Oh!"

He stretched his arms out into vacancy and folded them again quickly.

"I'd better go."

He stood up and walked several paces into the garden, where he feigned to be looking at the work she had left. Was he to break down now? Was the strength which he had relied on in so many temptations to fail him now, when his need was sorest?

In a few minutes he wheeled round to the bench and stopped full before her, no longer avoiding her eyes. She had taken up the book which he had laid on his end of the seat and was turning the pages.

"Have you read it?"

"Over and over."

"Ah! I knew I could trust you! You never disappoint. Sit down a little while."

"I'd - better go!"

"And haven't you a word? Bring this book back to me in silence? After all I said to you? I want to know how you feel about it - all your thoughts."

She looked up at him with a reproachful smile -

The blood had rushed guiltily into his face, and she seeing this, without knowing what it meant, the blood rushed into hers.

"I don't understand," she said proudly and coldly, dropping her eyes and dropping her head a little forward before him, and soon becoming very pale, as from a death-wound.

He stood before her, trembling, trying to speak, trying not to speak. Then he turned and strode rapidly away.

XVIII

THE next morning the parson was standing before his scant congregation of Episcopalians.

It was the first body of these worshippers gathered together in the wilderness mainly from the seaboard aristocracy of the Church of England. A small frame building on the northern slope of the wide valley served them for a meeting-house. No mystical half-lights there but the mystical half-lights of Faith; no windows but the many-hued windows of Hope; no arches but the vault of Love. What more did those men and women need in that land, over-shadowed always by the horror of quick or waiting death?

In addition to his meagre flock many an unclaimed goat of the world fell into that meek valley-path of Sunday mornings and came to hear, if not to heed, the voice of this quiet shepherd; so that now, as be stood delivering his final exhortation, his eyes ranged over wild, lawless, desperate countenances, rimming him darkly around. They glowered in at him through the door, where some sat upon the steps; others leaned in at the windows on each side of the room. Over the closely packed rough heads of these he could see others lounging further away on the grass beside their rifles, listening, laughing and talking. Beyond these stretched near fields green with maize, and cabins embosomed in orchards and gardens. Once a far-off band of children rushed across his field of vision, playing at Indian warfare and leaving in the bright air a cloud of dust from an old Indian war trail.

As he observed it all - this singularly mixed concourse of God-fearing men and women and of men and women who feared neither God nor man nor devil - as he beheld the young fields and the young children and the sweet transition of the whole land from bloodshed to innocence, the recollection of his mission in it and of the message of his Master brough out upon his cold, bleak, beautiful face the light of the Divine: so from a dark valley one may sometime have seen a snow-clad peak of the Alps lit up with the rays of the hidden sun.

He had chosen for his text the words "My peace I give unto you," and long before the closing sentences were reached, his voice was floating out with silvery, flute-like clearness on the still air of the summer morning, holding every soul, however unreclaimed, to intense and reverential silence:

"It is now twenty years since you scaled the mountains and hewed your path into this wilderness, never again to leave it. Since then you have known but war. As I look into your faces, I see the scar of many a wound; but more than the wounds I see are the wounds I do not see: of the body as well as of the spirit - the lacerations of sorrow, the strokes of bereavement. So that perhaps not one of you here but bears some brave visible or invisible sin of this awful past and of his share in the common strife. Twenty years are a long time to fight enemies of any kind, a long time to bold out against such as you have faced; and had you not been a mighty people sprung from the loins of a mighty race, no one

James Lane Allen

of you would be here this day to worship the God of your fathers in the faith of your fathers. The victory upon which you are entering at last is never the reward of the feeble, the cowardly, the faint-hearted. Out of your strength alone you have won your peace.

"But, O my brethren, while your land is now at peace, are you at peace? In the name of my Master, look each of you into his heart and answer: Is it not still a wilderness? full of the wild beasts of the appetites? the favourite hunting-ground of the passions? And is each of you, tried and faithful and fearless soldier that he may be on every other field, is each of you doing anything to conquer this?"

"My cry to-day then is the war-cry of the spirit. Subdue the wilderness within you! Step by step, little by little, as you have fought your way across this land from the Eastern mountains to the Western river, driven out every enemy and now hold it as your own, begin likewise to take possession of the other until in the end you may rule it also. If you are feeble; if fainthearted; if you do not bring into your lonely, silent, unwitnessed battles every virtue that you have relied on in this outward warfare of twenty years, you may never hope to come forth conquerors. By your strength, your courage, patience, watchfulness, constancy, - by the in-most will and beholden face of victory you are to overmaster the evil within yourselves as you have overmastered the peril in Kentucky."

"Then in truth you may dwell in green and tranquil pastures, where the will of God broods like summer light. Then you may come to realize the meaning of this promise of our Lord, 'My peace I give unto you': it is the gift of His peace to those alone who have learned to hold in quietness their land of the spirit."

White, cold, aflame with holiness, he stood before them; and every beholder, awe-stricken by the vision of that face, of a surety was thinking that this man's life was behind his speech: whether in ease or agony, he had found for his nature that victory of rest that was never to be taken from him.

But even as he stood thus, the white splendour faded from his countenance, leaving it shadowed with care. In one corner of the room, against the wall, shielding his face from the light of the window with his big black hat and the palm of his hand, sat the school-master. He was violently flushed, his eyes swollen and cloudy, his hair tossed, his linen rumpled, his posture bespeaking wretchedness and self-abandonment. Always in preaching the parson had looked for the face of his friend; always it had been his mainstay, interpreter, steadfast advocate in every plea for perfection of life. But to-day it had been kept concealed from him; nor until he had reached his closing exhortation, had the school-master once looked him in the eye, and he had done so then in a most remarkable manner: snatching the hat from before his face, straightening his big body up, and transfixing him with an expression of such resentment and reproach, that among all the wild faces before him, he could see none to match this one for disordered and evil passion. If he could have harboured a conviction so monstrous, he would have said that his words had pierced the owner of that face like a spear and that he was writhing under the torture.

As soon as he had pronounced the benediction he

James Lane Allen

looked toward the corner again, but the school-master had already left the room. Usually he waited until the others were gone and the two men walked homeward together, discussing the sermon.

To-day the others slowly scattered, and the parson sat alone at the tipper end of the room disappointed and troubled.

John strode up to the door.

"Are you ready?" he asked in a curt unnatural voice.

"Ah!" The parson sprang up gladly. "I was hoping you'd come!"

They started slowly off along the path, John walking unconsciously in it, the parson stumbling along through the grass and weeds on one side. It had been John's unvarying wont to yield the path to him.

"It is easy to preach," he muttered with gloomy, sarcastic emphasis.

"If you tried it once, you might think it easier to practise," retorted the parson, laughing.

"It might be easier to one who is not tempted."

"It might be easier to one who is. No man is tempted beyond his strength, but a sermon is often beyond his powers. I let you know, young man, that a homily may come harder than a virtue."

"How can you stand up and preach as you've been preaching, and then come out of the church and laugh about it!" cried John angrily.

"I'm not laughing about what I preached on," replied the parson with gentleness.

"You are in high spirits! You are gay! You are full of levity!"

"I am full of gladness. I am happy: is that a sin?"

John wheeled on him, stopping short, and pointing back to the church:

"Suppose there'd been a man in that room who was trying to some temptation - more terrible than you've ever known anything about. You'd made him feel that you were speaking straight at him - bidding him do right where it was so much easier to do wrong. You had helped him; he had waited to see you alone, hoping to get more help. Then suppose he had found you as you are now - full of your gladness! He wouldn't have believed in you! He'd have been hardened."

"If he'd been the right kind of man," replied the parson, quickly facing an arraignment had the rancour of denunciation, "he ought to have been more benefited by the sight of a glad man than the sound of a sad sermon. He'd have found in me a man who practises what he preaches: I have conquered my wilderness. But, I think," he added more gravely, "that if any such soul had come to me in his trouble, I could have helped him: if he had let me know what it was, he would have found that I could understand, could sympathize. Still, I don't see why you should condemn my conduct by the test of imaginary cases. I suppose I'm happy now because I'm glad to be with you," and the parson looked the school-master a little reproachfully in the eyes.

"And do you think I have no troubles?" said John, his lips trembling. He turned away and the parson walked beside him.

"You have two troubles to my certain knowledge," said he in the tone of one bringing forward a piece of critical analysis that was rather mortifying to exhibit. "The one is a woman and the other is John Calvin. If it's Amy, throw it off and be a man. If it's Calvinism, throw it off and become an Episcopalian." He laughed out despite himself.

"Did you ever love a woman?" asked John gruffly.

"Many a one - in the state of the first Adam!"

"That's the reason you threw it off: many a one!"

"Don't you know," inquired the parson with an air of exegetical candour, "that no man can be miserable because some woman or other has flirted his friend? That's the one trouble that every man laughs at - when it happens in his neighbourhood, not in his own house!"

The school-master made no reply.

"Or if it is Calvin," continued the parson, "thank God, I can now laugh at him, and so should you! Answer me one question: during the sermon, weren't you thinking of the case of a man born in a wilderness of temptations that he is foreordained never to conquer, and then foreordained to eternal damnation because he didn't conquer it?"

"No - no!"

"Well, you'd better've been thinking about it! For that's what you believe. And that's what makes life so hard and bitter and gloomy to you. I know! I carried Calvinism around within me once: it was like an uncorked ink-bottle in a rolling snowball: the farther you go, the blacker you get! Admit it now," he continued in his highest key of rarefied persistency, "admit that you were mourning over the babies in your school that will have to go to hell! You'd better be getting some of your own: the Lord will take care of other people's! Go to see Mrs. Falconer! See all you can of her. There's a woman to bring you around!"

They had reached the little bridge over the clear, swift Elkhorn. Their paths diverged. John stopped at his companion's last words, and stood looking at him with some pity.

"I thank you for your sermon," he said huskily; "I hope to get some help from that. But you! - you are making things harder for me every word you utter. You don't understand and I can't tell you."

He took the parson's cool delicate hand in his big hot one.

Alone in the glow of the golden dusk of that day he was sitting outside his cabin on the brow of the hill, overlooking the town in the valley. How peaceful it lay in the Sunday evening light! The burden of the parson's sermon weighed more heavily than ever on his spirit. He had but to turn his eye down the valley and there, flashing in the sheen of sunset, flowed the great spring, around the margin of which the first group of Western hunters had camped for the night and given the place its name from one of the battle-fields of the Revolution; up the valley he could see the roof under which the Virginia aristocracy of the Church of England had consecrated their first poor shrine. What history lay between the finding of that spring and the building of that altar! Not the winning of the wilderness simply; not alone its peace. That westward penetrating wedge of iron-browed, iron-muscled, iron-hearted men, who were now beginning to be known as the Kentuckians, had not only cleft a road for themselves; they had opened a fresh highway for the tread of the nation and found a vaster heaven for the Star of Empire. Already this youthful gigantic West was beginning to make its voice heard from Quebec to New Orleans while beyond the sea the three greatest kingdoms of Europe had grave and troubled thoughts of the on-rushing power it foretokened and the unimaginably splendid future for the Anglo-Saxon race that it forecast.

He recalled the ardour with which he had followed the tramp of those wild Westerners; footing it alone from the crest of the Cumberland; subsisting on the game he could kill by the roadside; sleeping at night on his rifle in some thicket of underbrush or cane; resolute to make his way to this new frontier of the new republic in the new world; open his school, read law, and begin his practice, and cast his destiny in with its heroic people.

And now this was the last Sunday in a long time, perhaps forever, that he should see it all - the valley, the town, the evening land, resting in its peace. Before the end of another week his horse would be climbing the ranges of the Alleghanies, bearing him on his way to Mount Vernon and thence to Philadelphia. By outward compact he was going on one mission for the Transylvania Library Committee and on another from his Democratic Society to the political Clubs of the East. But in his own soul he knew he was going likewise because it would give him the chance to fight his own battle out, alone and far away.

Fight it out here, he felt that he never could. He could neither live near her and not see her, nor see her and not betray the truth. His whole life had been a protest against the concealment either of his genuine dislikes or his genuine affections. How closely he had come to the tragedy of a confession, she to the tragedy of an understanding, the day before! Her deathly pallor had haunted him ever since - that look of having suffered a terrible wound. Perhaps she understood already.

Then let her understand! Then at least he could go away better satisfied: if he never came back, she would know: every year of that long separation, her mind would be bearing him the pardoning companionship that every woman must yield the man who has loved her, and still loves her, wrongfully and hopelessly: of itself that knowledge would be a great deal to him during all those years.

Struggle against it as he would, the purpose was steadily gaining ground within him to see her and if she did not now know everything then to tell her the truth. The consequences would be a tragedy, but might it not be a tragedy of another kind? For there were darker moments when he probed strange recesses of life for him in the possibility that his confession might open up a like confession from her. He had once believed Amy to be true when she was untrue. Might he not be deceived here? Might she not appear true, but in reality be untrue? If he were successfully concealing his love from her, might she not be successfully concealing her love from him? And if they found each other out, what then?

At such moments all through him like an alarm bell sounded her warning: "The only things that need trouble us very much are not the things it is right to conquer but the things it is wrong to conquer. If you ever conquer anything in yourself that is right, that will be a real trouble for you as long as you live - and for me!"

Had she meant this? But whatever mood was uppermost, of one thing he now felt assured: that the sight of her made his silence more difficult. He had fancied that her mere presence, her purity, her constancy, her loftiness of nature would rebuke and rescue him from the evil in himself: it had only stamped upon this the consciousness of reality. He had never even realized until he saw her the last time how beautiful she was; the change in himself had opened his eyes to this; and her greater tenderness toward him in their talk of his departure, her dependence on his friendship, her coming loneliness, the sense of a tragedy in her life - all these sweet half-mute appeals to sympathy and affection had rioted in his memory every moment since.

Therefore it befell that the parson's sermon of the morning had dropped like living coals on his conscience. It had sounded that familiar, lifelong, best-loved, trumpet call of duty - the old note of joy in his strength rightly and valiantly to be put forth - which had always kindled him and had always been his boast. All the afternoon those living coals of divine remonstrance had been burning into him deeper and deeper but in vain: they could only torture, not persuade. For the first time in his life he had met face to face the fully aroused worst passions of his own stubborn, defiant, intractable nature: they too loved victory and were saying they would have it.

One by one the cabins disappeared in the darkness. One by one the stars bloomed out yellow in their still meadows. Over the vast green sea of the eastern wilderness the moon swung her silvery lamp, and up the valley floated a wide veil of mist bedashed with silvery light.

The parson climbed the crest of the hill, sat down, laid his hat on the grass, and slipped his long sensitive fingers backward over his shining hair. Neither man spoke at first; their friendship put them at ease. Nor did the one notice the shrinking and dread which was the other's only welcome.

"Did you see the Falconers this morning?"

The parson's tone was searching and troubled and gentler than it had been earlier that day.

"No."

"They were looking for you. They thought you'd gone home and said they'd go by for you. They expected you to go out with them to dinner. Haven't you been there to-day?"

"No."

"I certainly supposed you'd go. I know they looked for you and must have been disappointed. Isn't this your last Sunday?"

"Yes."

He answered absently. He was thinking that if she was looking for him, then she had not understood and their relation still rested on the old innocent footing. Whatever explanation of his conduct and leave-taking the day before she had devised, it had not been in his disfavour. In all probability, she had referred it, as she had referred everything else, to his affair with Amy. His conscience smote him at the thought of her indestructible trust in him.

"If this is your last Sunday," resumed the parson in a voice rather plaintive, "then this is our last Sunday night together. And that was my last sermon. Well, it's not a bad one to take with you. By the time you get back, you'll thank me more for it than you did this morning - if you heed it."

There was another silence before he continued, musingly:

"What an expression a sermon will sometimes bring out on a man's face! While I was preaching, I saw many a thing that no man knew I saw. It was as though I were crossing actual wilderness-es; I met the wild beasts of different souls, I crept up on the lurking savages of the passions. I believe some of those men would have liked to confess to me. I wish they had."

He forbore to speak of John's black look, though it was of this that he was most grievously thinking and would have led the way to have explained. But no answer came."

There was one face with no hidden guilt in it, no shame. I read into the depths of that clear mind. It said: 'I have conquered my wilderness.' I have never known another such woman as Mrs. Falconer. She never speaks of herself; but when I am with her, I feel that the struggles of my life have been nothing."

"Yes," he continued, out of kindness trying to take no notice of his companion's silence, "she holds in quietness her land of the spirit; but there are battle-fields in her nature that fill me with awe by their silence. I'd dread to be the person to cause her any further trouble in this world."

The schoolmaster started up, went into the cabin, and quickly came out again. The parson, absorbed in his reflections, had not noticed:

"You've thought I've not sympathized with you in your affair with Amy. It's true. But if you'd ever loved this woman and failed, I could have sympathized."

"Why don't you raise the money to build a better church by getting up a lottery?" asked John, breaking in harshly upon the parson's gentleness.

The question brought on a short discussion of this method of aiding schools and churches, then much in vogue. The parson rather favoured the plan (and it is known that afterwards a better church was built for him through this device); but his companion bore but a listless part in the talk: he was balancing the chances, the honour and the dishonour, in a lottery of life.

"You are not like yourself to-day," said the parson reproachfully after silence had come on again.

I know it," replied John freely, as if awaking at last.

"Well, each of us has his troubles. Sometimes I have likened the human race to a caravan of camels crossing a desert - each with sore on his hump and each with his load so placed as to rub that sore. It is all right for the back to bear its burden, but I don't think there should have been any sore!"

"Let me ask you a question," said John, suddenly and earnestly. "Have there ever been days in your life when, if you'd been the camel, you'd have thrown the load and driver off?"

"Ah!" said the parson keenly, but gave no answer.

"Have there ever been days when you'd rather have done wrong than right?"

"Yes; there have been such days - when I was young and wild." The confession was reluctant.

"Have you ever had a trouble, and everybody around you fell upon you in the belief that it was something else?"

"That has happened to me - I suppose to all of us."

"Were you greatly helped by their misunderstanding you?"

"I can't say that I was."

"You would have been glad for them to know the truth, but you didn't choose to tell them?"

"Yes; I have gone through such an experience."

"So that their sympathy was in effect ridiculous?"

"That is true also."

"If you have been through all this," said John conclusively, "then without knowing anything more, you can understand why I am not like myself, as you say, and haven't been lately."

The parson moved his chair over beside the schoolmaster's and took one of his hands in both of his own, drawing it into his lap.

"John," he said with affection, "I've been wrong: forgive me! And I can respect your silence. But don't let anything come between us and keep it from me. One question now on this our last Sunday night together: Have you anything against me in this world?"

"Not one thing! Have you anything against me?"

"Not one thing!"

Neither spoke for a while. Then the parson resumed:

"I not only have nothing against you, but I've something to say; we might never meet hereafter. You remember the woman who broke the alabaster box for the feet of the Saviour while he was living - that most beautiful of all the appreciations? And you know what we do? Let our fellow-beings carry their crosses to their Calvarys, and after each has suffered his agony and entered into his peace, we go out to him and break our alabaster boxes above his stiff cold feet. I have always hoped that my religion might enable me to break my alabaster box for the living who alone can need it - and who always do need it. Here is mine for your feet, John: Of all the men I have ever known, you are the most sincere; of them all I would soonest pick upon you to do what is right; of them all you have the cleanest face, because you have the most innocent heart; of them all you have the highest notions of what a man may do and be in this life. I have drawn upon your strength ever since I knew you. You have a great deal. It is fortunate; you will need a great deal; for the world will always be a battle-field to you, but the victory will be worth the fighting. And my last words to you are: fight it out to the end; don't compromise with evil; don't lower your ideals or your aims. If it can be any help to you to know it, I shall always be near you in spirit when you are in trouble; if you ever need me, I will come; and if my poor prayers can ever bring you a blessing, you shall have that."

The parson turned his calm face up toward the firmament and tears glistened in his eyes. Then perhaps from the old habit and need of following a sermon with a hymn, he said quite simply:

"Would you like a little music? It is the Good-bye of the Flute to you and a pleasant journey."

The school-master's head had dropped quickly upon his arms, which were crossed over the back of his chair. While the parson was praising him, he had put out his hand two or three times with wretched, imploring gestures. Keeping his face still hidden, he moved his head now in token of assent; and out upon the stillness of the night floated the Farewell of the Flute.

But no sermon, nor friendship, nor music, nor voice of conscience, nor voice of praise, nor ideals, nor any other earthly thing could stand this day against the evil that was in him. The parson had scarce gone away through the misty beams before he sprang up and seized his hat.

There was no fog out on the clearing. He could not have said why he had come. He only knew that he was there in the garden where he had parted from her the day before. He sat on the bench where they had talked so often, he strolled among her plants. How clear in the moonlight every leaf of the dark green little things was, many of them holding white drops of dew on their tips and edges! How plain the last shoe-prints where she had worked! How peaceful the whole scene in every direction, how sacredly at rest! And the cabin up there at the end of the garden where they were sleeping side by side - how the moon poured its strongest light upon that: his eye could never get away from it. So closely a man might live with a woman in this seclusion! So entirely she must be his!

His passions leaped like dogs against their chains when brought too near. They began to draw him toward the cabin until at last he had come opposite to it, his figure remaining hidden behind the fence and under the heavy shadow of a group of the wilderness trees. Then it was that taking one step further, he drew back.

The low window of the cabin was open and she was sitting there near the foot of her bed, perfectly still and looking out into the night. Her face rested in one palm, her elbow on the window sill. Her nightgown had slipped down from her arm. The only sleepless thing in all the peace of that summer night: the yearning image of mated loneliness.

He was so close that he could hear the loud regular breathing of a sleeper on the bed just inside the shadow. Once the breathing stopped abruptly; and a moment later, as though in reply to a command, he heard her say without turning her head:

"I am coming!"

The voice was sweet and dutiful; but to an ear that could have divined everything, so dead worn away with weariness.

Then he saw an arm put forth. Then he heard the shutter being fastened on the inside.

XIX

THE closing day of school had come; and although he had waited in impatience for the end, it was with a lump in his throat that he sat behind the desk and ruler for the last time and looked out on the gleeful faces of the children. No more toil and trouble between them and him from this time on; a dismissal, and as far as he was concerned the scattering of the huddled lambkins to the wide pastures and long cold mountain sides of the world. He had grown so fond of them and he had grown so used to teach them by talking to them, that his speech overflowed. But it had been his unbroken wont to keep his troubles out of the schoolroom; and although the thought never left him of the other parting to be faced that day, he spoke out bravely and cheerily, with a smile:

"This is the last day of school, and you know that to-morrow I am going away and may never come back. Whether I do or not, I shall never teach again, so that I am now saying good-bye to you for life.

"What I wish to impress upon you once more is the kind of men and women your fathers and mothers were and the kind of men and women you must become to be worthy of them. I am not speaking so much to those of you whose parents have not been long in Kentucky as to those whose parents were the first to fight for the land until it was safe for others to follow and share it. Let me tell you that nothing like that was ever done before in all this world. And if, as I sit here, I can't help seeing that this one of you has no father and this one no mother and this one neither father nor mother and that almost none of you have both, still I cannot help saying, You ought to be happy children! not that you have lost your parents, but that you have had such parents to lose and to remember!

"All of you are still too young to know fully what they have done and how the whole world will some day speak of them. Still, you can understand some things. For nowadays, when you go to your homes at night, you can lie down and sleep without fear or danger.

"And in the mornings your fathers go off to the fields to their work, your mothers go off to theirs, you go off to yours, feeling sure that you will all come together at night again. Some of you can remember when this was not so. Your father would put his arms around you in the morning and you would never see him again; your mother kissed you, and waved her hand to you as she went out of the gate; and you never knew what became of her afterwards.

"And don't you recollect how you little babes in the wilderness could never go anywhere? If you heard wild turkeys gobbling just inside the forest, or an owl hooting, or a paroquet screaming, or a fawn bleating, you were warned never to go there; it was the trick of the Indians. You could never go near a clump of high weeds, or a patch of cane, or a stump, or a fallen tree. You must not go to the sugar camp, to get a good drink, or to a salt lick for a pinch of salt, or to the field for an ear of corn, or even to the spring for a bucket of water: so that you could have neither bread nor water nor sugar nor salt. Always, always, it was the Indians. If you cried in the night, your mother came over to you and whispered 'Hush! they are coming! They will get you!' And you forgot your pain and clung to her neck and listened.

"Now you are let alone, you go farther and farther away from your homes, you can play hide-and-seek in the canebrakes, you can explore the woods, you fish and you hunt, you are free for the land is safe.

"And then only think, that by the time you are men and women, Kentucky will no longer be the great wilderness it still is. There will be thousands and thousands of people scattered over it; and the forest will be cut down - can you ever believe that? - cut through and through, leaving some trees here and some trees there. And the cane will be cut down: can you believe that? And instead of buffalo and wild-cats and bears and wolves and panthers there will be flocks of the whitest sheep, with little lambs frisking about on the green spring meadows. And under the big shady trees in the pastures there will be herds of red cattle, so gentle and with backs so soft and broad that you could almost stretch yourselves out and go to sleep on them, and they would never stop chewing their cuds. Only think of the hundreds of orchards with their apple-blossoms and of the big ripe, golden apples on the trees in the fall! It will be one of the quietest, gentlest lands that a people ever owned; and this is the gift of your fathers who fought for it and of your mothers who fought for it also. And you must never forget that you would never have had such fathers, had you not had such mothers to stand by them and to die with them.

James Lane Allen

"This is what I have wished to teach you more than anything in your books - that you may become men and women worthy of them and of what they have left you. But while being the bravest kind of men and women, you should try also to be gentle men and gentle women. You boys must get over your rudeness and your roughness; that is all right in you now but it would be all wrong in you afterwards. And the last and the best thing I have to say to you is be good boys and grow up to be good men! That sounds very plain and common but I can wish you nothing better for there is nothing better. As for my little girls, they are good enough as they are!

"I have talked a long time. God bless you everyone. I wish you long and happy lives and I hope we may meet again. And now all of you must come and shake hands with me and tell me good-bye."

They started forward and swarmed toward him; only, as the foremost of them rose and hid her from sight, little Jennie, with one mighty act of defiant joy, hurled her arithmetic out of the window; and a chubby-cheeked veteran on the end of the bench produced a big red apple from between his legs and went for it with a smack of gastric rapture that made his toes curl and sent his glance to the rafters. They swarmed on him, and he folded his arms around the little ones and kissed them; the older boys, the warriors, brown and barefoot, stepping sturdily forward one by one, and holding out a strong hand that closed on his and held it, their eyes answering his sometimes with clear calm trust and fondness, sometimes lowered and full of tears; other little hands resting unconsciously on each of his shoulders, waiting for their turns. Then there were softened echoes - gay voices, dying away in one direction and another, and then - himself alone in the room - school-master no longer.

He waited till there was silence, sitting in his old erect way behind his desk, the bight smile still on his face though his eyes were wet. Then, with the thought that now he was to take leave of her, he suddenly leaned forward and buried his face on his arms.

XX

IN the Country of the Spirit there is a certain high table-land that lies far on among the out-posts toward Eternity. Standing on that calm clear height, where the sun shines ever though it shines coldly, the wayfarer may look behind him at his own footprints of self-renunciation, below on his dark zones of storm, and forward to the final land where the mystery, the pain, and the yearning of his life will either be infinitely satisfied or infinitely quieted. But no man can write a description of this place for those who have never trodden it; by those who have, no description is desired: their fullest speech is Silence. For here dwells the Love of which there has never been any confession, from which there is no escape, for which there is no hope: the love of a man for a woman who is bound to another, or the love of a woman for a man who is bound to another. Many there are who know what that means, and this is the reason why the land is always thronged. But in the throng no one signals another; to walk there is to be counted among the Unseen and the Alone.

To this great wistful height of Silence he had struggled at last after all his days of rising and falling, of climbing and slipping back. It was no especial triumph for his own strength. His better strength had indeed gone into it, and the older rightful habitudes of mind that always mean so much to us when we are tried and tempted, and the old beautiful submission of himself to the established laws of the world. But more than what these had effected was what she herself had been to him and had done for him. Even his discovery of her at the window that last night had had the effect of bidding him stand off; for he saw there the loyalty and sacredness of wifehood that, however full of suffering, at least asked for itself the privilege and the dignity of suffering unnoticed.

Thus he had come to realize that life had long been leading him blindfold, until one recent day, snatching the bandage from his eyes, she had cried: "Here is the parting of three ways, each way a tragedy: choose your way and your tragedy!"

If he confessed his love and found that she felt but friendship for him, there was the first tragedy. The wrong in him would lack the answering wrong in her, which sometimes, when the two are put together, so nearly makes up the right. From her own point of view, he would merely be offering her a delicate ineffaceable insult. If she had been the sort of woman by whose vanity every conquest is welcomed as a tribute and pursued as an aim, he could never have cared for her at all. Thus while his love took its very origin from his belief of her nobility, he was premeditating the means of having her prove to him that this did not exist.

If he told her everything and surprised her love for him, there was the second tragedy. For over there, beyond the scene of such a confession, he could not behold her as anything else than a fatally lowered woman. The agony of this, even as a possibil-ity, overwhelmed him in advance. To require of her that she should have a nature of perfect loyalty and at the same time to ask her to pronounce her own falseness - what happiness could that bring to him? If she could be faithless to one man because she loved another, could she not be false to the second, if in time she grew to love a third? Out of the depths even of his loss of her the terrible cry was wrung from him that no love could long be possible between him and any woman who was not free to love him.

And so at last, with that mingling of selfish and unselfish motives, which is like the mixed blood of the heart itself, he had chosen the third tragedy: the silence that would at least leave each of them blameless. And so he had come finally to that high cold table-land where the sun of Love shines rather as the white luminary of another world than the red quickener of this.

Over the lofty table-land of Kentucky the sky bent darkest blue, and was filled with wistful, silvery light that afternoon as he walked out to the Falconers'. His face had never looked so clear, so calm; his very linen never so spotless, or so careful about his neck and wrists; and his eyes held again their old beautiful light - saddened.

From away off he could descry her, walking about the yard in the pale sunshine. He had expected to find her preoccupied as usual; but to-day she was strolling restlessly to and fro in front of the house, quite near it and quite idle. When she saw him coming, scarce aware of her own actions, she went round the house and walked on quickly away from him.

As he was following and passing the cabin, a hand was

quickly put out and the shutter drawn partly to.

"How do you do!"

That hard, smooth, gay little voice!

"You mustn't come here! And don't you peep! When are you going?"

He told her.

"To-morrow! Why, have you forgotten that I'm married to-morrow! Aren't you coming? Upon my word! I've given you to the widow Babcock, and you are to ride in the procession with her. She has promised me not to laugh once on the way or even to allude to anything cheerful! Be persuaded! . . . Well, I'm sorry. I'll have to give your place to Peter, I suppose. And I'll tell the widow she can be natural and gay: Peter'll not mind! Good-bye! I can't shake hands with you."

Behind the house, at the foot of the sloping hill, there was a spring such as every pioneer sought to have near his home; and a little lower down, in one corner of the yard, the water from this had broadened out into a small pond. Dark-green sedgy cane grew thick around half the margin.

One March day some seasons before, Major Falconer had brought down with his rifle from out the turquoise sky a young lone-wandering swan. In those early days the rivers and ponds of the wilderness served as resting places and feeding-grounds for these unnumbered birds in their long flights between the Southern waters and the Northern lakes. A wing of this one had been broken, and out of her wide heaven of freedom and

James Lane Allen

light she had floated down his captive but with all her far-sweeping instincts throbbing on unabated. This pool had been the only thing to remind her since of the blue-breasted waves and the glad fellowship of her kind. On this she had passed her existence, with a cry in the night now and then that no one heard, a lifting of the wings that would never rise, an eye turned upward toward the turquoise sky across which familiar voices called to each other, called down, and were lost in the distance.

As he followed down the hill, she was standing on the edge of the pond, watching the swan feeding in the edge of the cane. He took her hand without a word, and looked with clear unfaltering eyes down into her face, now swanlike in whiteness.

She withdrew her hand and gave him the gloves which she was holding in the other.

"I'm glad you thought enough of them to come for them."

"I couldn't come! Don't blame me!"

"I understand! Only I might have helped you in your trouble. If a friend can't do that - may not do that! But it is too late now! You start for Virginia tomorrow?"

"To-morrow."

"And to-morrow Amy marries, I lose you both the same day! You are going straight to Mount Vernon?"

"Straight to Mount Vernon."

"Ah, to think that you will see Virginia so soon! I've been recalling a great deal about Virginia during these days when you would not come to see me. Now I've forgotten everything I meant to say!"

They climbed the hill slowly. Two or three times she stopped and pressed her hand over her heart. She tried to hide the sound of her quivering breath and glanced up once to see whether he were observing. He was not. With his old habit of sending his thoughts on into the future, fighting its distant battles, feeling its far-off pain, he was less conscious of their parting than of the years during which he might not see her again. It is the woman who bursts the whole grape of sorrow against the irrepressible palate at such a moment; to a man like him the same grape distils a vintage of yearning that will brim the cup of memory many a time beside his lamp in the final years.

He would have passed the house, supposing they were to go to the familiar seat in the garden; but a bench had been placed under a forest tree near the door and she led the way to this. The significance of the action was lost on him.

"Yes," she continued, returning to a subject which furnished both an escape and a concealment of her feelings, "I have been revisiting my girlhood. You love Kentucky but I cannot make myself over."

Her face grew full of the finest memories and all the fibres of her nature were becoming more unstrung. He had made sure of his strength before he had ever dared see her this day, had pitted his self-control against every possible temptation to betray himself that could arise throughout their parting; and it was this very composure, so unlocked for, that unconsciously drove her to the opposite extreme. Shades of colour swept over her neck and brow, as though she were setting under wind-tossed blossoming peach boughs. Her lustrous, excited eyes seemed never able to withdraw themselves from his whitened solemn face. Its mute repressed suffering touched her; its calmness filled her with vague pain that at such a time he could be so calm. And the current of her words ran swift, as a stream loosened at last from some steep height. "Sometime you might be in that part of Virginia. I should like you to know the country there and the place where my father's house stood. And when you see the Resident, I wish you would recall my father to him. And you remember that one of my brothers was a favourite young officer of his. I should like you to hear him speak of them both: he has not forgotten. Ah! My father! He had his faults, but they were all the faults of a gentleman. And the faults of my brothers were the faults of gentlemen. I never saw my mother; but I know how genuine she was by the books she liked and her dresses and her jewels, and the manner in which she had things put away in the closets. One's childhood is everything! If I had not felt I was all there was in the world to speak for my father and my mother and my brothers! Ah, sometimes pride is the greatest of virtues!"

He bowed his head in assent.

With a swift transition she changed her voice and manner and the conversation: "That is enough about me. Have you thought that you will soon be talking to the greatest man in the world - you who love ideals?"

"I have not thought of it lately."

"You will think of it soon! And that reminds me: why did you go away as you did the last time you were here - when I wanted to talk with you about the book?"

Her eyes questioned him imperiously. "I cannot tell you: that is one of the things you'd better not wish to understand.

She continued to look at him, and when she spoke, her voice was full of relief: "It was the first time you ever did anything that I could not understand: I could not read your face that day." "Can you read it now?" he asked, smiling at her sorrowfully. "Perfectly!"

"What do you read?"

"Everything that I have always liked you for most. Memories are a great deal to me. Ah, if you had ever done anything to spoil yours!" Do you think that if I loved a woman she would know it by looking at my face?" "You would tell her: that is your nature."

"Would I? Should I?"

"Why not?" There was silence. "Let me talk to you about the book," he cried suddenly. He closed his eyes and passed one hand several times slowly across his forehead; then facing her but with his arm resting on the back of the seat and his eyes shaded by his hand he began:

"You were right: it is a book I have needed. At first it appeared centuries old to me and far away: the greatest gorgeous picture I had ever seen of human life anywhere. I could never tell you of the regret with which it filled me not to have lived in those days - of the longing to have been at Camelot to have seen the King and to have served him; to have been friends with the best of the Knights; to have taken their vows; to have gone out with them to right what was wrong, to wrong nothing that was right."

The words were wrung from him with slow terrible effort, as though he were forcing himself to draw nearer and nearer some spot of supreme mental struggle. She listened, stilled, as she had never been by any words of his. At the same time she felt stifled - felt that she should have to cry out - that he could be so deeply moved and so self-controlled.

More slowly, with more composure, he went on. He was still turned toward her, his hand shading the upper part of his face:

"It was not until - not until - afterwards - that I got something more out of it than all that - got what I suppose you meant. . . . suppose you meant that the whole story was not far away from me but present here - its right and wrong - its temptation; that there was no vow a man could take then that a man must not take now; that every man still has his Camelot and his King, still has to prove his courage and his strength to all men . . . and that after he has proved these, he has - as his last, highest act of service in the world. . . to lay them all down, give them all up, for the sake of - of his spirit. You meant that I too, in my life, am to go in quest of the Grail: is it all that?"

The tears lay mute on her eyes. She rose quickly and walked away to the garden. He followed her. When they had entered it, he strolled beside her among the plants.

"You must see them once more," she said. Her tone was perfectly quiet and careless. Then she continued with animation: "Some day you will not know this garden. When we are richer, you will see what I shall do: with it, with the house, with everything! I do not live altogether on memories: I have hopes."

They came to the bench where they were used to talk, She sat down, and waited until she could control the least tremor of her voice. Then she turned upon him her noble eyes, the exquisite passionate tender light of which no effort of the will could curtain in. Nor could any self-restraint turn aside the electrical energy of her words:"I thought I should not let you go away without saying something more to you about what has happened lately with Amy. My interest in you, your future, your success, has caused me to feel everything more than you can possibly realize. But I am not thinking of this now: it is nothing, it will pass. What it has caused me to see and to regret more than anything else is the power that life will have to hurt you on account of the ideals that you have built up in secret. We have been talking about Sir Thomas Malory and chivalry and ideals: there is one thing you need to know - all of us need to know it - and to know it well."Ideals are of two kinds. There are those that correspond to our highest sense of perfection. They express what we might be were life, the world, ourselves, all different, all better. Let these be high as they may! They are not useless because unattainable. Life is not a failure because they are never attained. God Himself requires of us the unattainable: 'Be ye perfect, even as I am perfect! He could not do less. He commands perfection, He forgives us that we are not perfect! Nor does He count us failures because we have to be forgiven. Our ideals also demand of us perfection - the impossible; but because we come far short of this we have no right to count ourselves as failures. What are they like - ideals such as these? They are like light-houses. But light-houses are not made to live in; neither can we live in such ideals. I suppose they are meant to shine on us from afar, when the sea of our life is dark and stormy, perhaps to remind us of a haven of hope, as we drift or sink in shipwreck. All of your ideals are lighthouses. "But there are ideals of another sort; it is these that you lack. As we advance into life, out of larger experience of the world and of ourselves, are unfolded the ideals of what will be possible to us if we make the best use of the world and of ourselves, taken as we are. Let these be as high as they may, they will always be lower than those others which are perhaps the veiled intimations of our immortality. These will always be imperfect; but life is not a failure because they are so. It is these that are to burn for us, not like light-houses in the distance, but like candles in our hands. For so many of us they are too much like candles! - the longer they burn, the lower they burn, until before death they go out altogether! But I know that it will not be thus with you. At first you will have disappoint-ments and suffer-ings - the world on one side, unattainable ideals of perfection on the other. But by degrees the comforting light of what you may actually do and be in an imperfect world will shine close to you and all around you, more and more. It is this that will lead you never to perfection, but always toward it."

He bowed his head: the only answer he could make.

It was getting late. The sun at this moment passed behind the western tree-tops. It was the old customary signal for him to go. They suddenly looked at each other in that shadow. "I shall always think of you for your last words to me," he said in a thick voice, rising. "Some day you will find the woman who will be a candle," she replied sadly, rising also. Then with her lips trembling, she added piteously:

"Oh, if you ever marry, don't make the mistake of treating the woman as an ideal Treat her in every way as a human being exactly like yourself! With the same weakness, the same strug-les, the same temptations! And as you have some mercy on yourself despite your faults, have some mercy on her despite hers."

"Must I ever think of you as having been weak and tempted as I have been?" he cried, the guilty blood rushing into his face in the old struggle to tell her everything. "Oh, as for me - what do you know of me!" she cried, laughing. And then more quickly: "I have read your face! What do you read in mine?" He looked long into it: "All that I have most wished to see in the face of any woman - except one thing!" "What is that? But don't tell me!"

She turned away toward the garden gate. In silence they passed out - walking toward the edge of the clearing. Half-way she paused. He lifted his hat and held out his hand. She laid hers in it and they gave each other the long clinging grasp of affection."Always be a good man," she said, tightening her grasp and turning her face away.

As he was hurrying off, she called to him in a voice full of emotion:

"Come back!"

He wheeled and walked towards her blindly.

She scanned his face, feature by feature.

"Take off your hat!" she said with a tremulous little laugh. He did so and she looked at his forehead and his hair.

"Go now, dear friend!" she said calmly but quickly.

XXI

It was the morning of the wedding.

According to the usage of the time the marriage ceremony was to take place early in the forenoon, in order that the guests, gathered in from distant settlements of the wilderness, might have a day for festivity and still reach home before night. Late in the afternoon the bridal couple, escorted by many friends, were to ride into town to Joseph's house, and in the evening there was to be a house-warming.

The custom of the backwoods country ran that a man must not be left to build his house alone; and one day some weeks before this wagons had begun to roll in from this direction and that direction out of the forest, hauling the logs for Joseph's cabin. Then with loud laughter and the writhing of tough backs and the straining of powerful arms and legs, men old, middle-aged, and young had raised the house like overgrown boys at play, and then had returned to their own neglected business: so that to him was left only the finishing. He had finished it and furnished it for the simple scant needs of pioneer life.But on this, his wedding morning, he had hardly left the town, escorted by friends on horseback, before many who had variously excused themselves from going began to issue from their homes: women carrying rolls of linen

James Lane Allen

and pones of bread; boys with huge joints of jerked meat and dried tongues of the buffalo, bear, and deer. There was a noggin, a piggin, a churn, a homemade chair; there was a quilt from a grandmother and a pioneer cradle - a mere trough scooped out of a walnut log. An old pioneer sent the antlers of a stag for a hat-rack, and a buffalo rug for the young pair to lie warm under of bitter, winter nights; his wife sent a spinning-wheel and a bundle of shingles for johnny-cakes. Some of the merchants gave packages of Philadelphia groceries; some of the aristo-cratic families parted with heirlooms that had been laboriously brought over the mountains - a cup and saucer of Sevres, a pair of tall brass candlesticks, and a Venus - mirror framed in ebony. It was about three o'clock in the afternoon when John Gray jumped on the back of a strong trusty horse at the stable of the Indian Queen, leaned over to shake the hands of the friends who had met there to see him off, and turned his horse's head in the direction of the path that led to the Wilderness Road.

But when he had gone about a mile, he struck into the forest at right angles and rode across the country until he reached that green woodland pathway which led from the home of the Falconers to the public road between Lexington and Frankfort. He tied his horse some distance away, and walking back, sat down on the roots of an oak and waited.

It was a day when the beauty of the earth makes itself felt like ravishing music that has no sound. The air, warm and full of summer fragrance, was of that ethereal untinged clearness which spreads over all things the softness of velvet. The far-vaulted heavens, so bountiful of light, were an illimitable weightless curtain of pale-blue velvet; the rolling clouds were of white velvet; the grass, the stems of bending wild flowers, the drooping sprays of woodland foliage, were so many forms of emerald velvet; the gnarled trunks of the trees were gray and brown velvet; the wings and breasts of the birds, flitting hither and thither, were of gold and scarlet velvet; the butterflies were stemless, floating velvet blossoms."Farewell, Kentucky! Farewell!" he said, looking about him at it all. Two hours passed. The shadows were lengthening rapidly. Over the forest, like the sigh of a spirit, swept from out the west the first intimation of waning light, of the mysteries of coming darkness. At last there reached his ear from far down the woodland path the sounds of voices and laughter - again and again - louder and louder - and then through the low thick boughs he caught glimpses of them coming. Now beneath the darker arches of the trees, now across pale-green spaces shot by slanting sunbeams. Once there was a halt and a merry outcry. Long grape-vines from opposite sides of the road had been tied across it, and this barrier had to cut through. Then on they came again: At the head of procession, astride an old horse that in his better days had belonged to a mounted rifleman, rode the parson. He was several yards ahead of the others and quite forgetful of them. The end of his flute stuck neglectedly out of his waistcoat pocket; his bridle reins lay slack on the neck of the drowsy beast; his hands were piled on the pommel of the saddle as over his familiar pulpit; his dreamy moss-agate eyes were on the tree-tops far ahead. In truth he was preparing a sermon on the affection of one man for another and ransacking Scripture for illustrations; and he meant to preach this the following Sunday when there would be some one sadly missed among his hearers. Nevertheless he enjoyed great peace of spirit this day: it was not John who rode behind him as the

James Lane Allen

bridegroom: otherwise he would as soon have returned to the town at the head of the forces of Armageddon.

Behind the parson came William Penn in the glory of a new bridle and saddle and a blanket of crimson cloth; his coat smooth as satin, his mane a tumbling cataract of white silk; bunches of wild roses at his ears; his blue-black eyes never so soft, and seeming to lift his feet cautiously like an elephant bearing an Indian princess.

They were riding side by side, the young husband and wife. He keeping one hand on the pommel of her saddle, thus holding them together; while with the other he used his hat to fan his face, now hers, though his was the one that needed it, she being cool and quietly radiant with the thoughts of her triumph that day - the triumph of her wedding, of her own beauty. Furthermore show was looking ahead to the house-warming that night when she would be able to triumph again and also count her presents.

Then came Major and Mrs. Falconer. Her face was hidden by a veil and as they passed, it was held turned toward him: he was talking, uninterrupted.

Then followed Horatio Turpin and Kitty Poythress; and then Erskine and his betrothed, he with fresh feathers of the hawk and the scarlet tanager gleaming in his cap above his swart, stern aquiline face. Then Peter, beside the widow Babcock; he openly aflame and solicitous; she coy and discreetly inviting, as is the wisdom of some. Then others and others and others - a long gay pageant, filling the woods with merry voices and laughter.

They passed and the sounds died away - passed on to the town awaiting the, to the house-warming, and please God, to long life and some real affection and happiness.

Once he had expected to ride beside her at the head of this procession. There had gone by him the vision of his own life as it was to have been.

Long after the last sound had ceased in the distance he was sitting at the root of the red oak. The sun set, the moon rose, he was there still. A loud, impatient neigh from his horse aroused him. He sprang lightly up, meaning to ride all night and not to draw rein until he had crossed the Kentucky River and reached Traveller's Rest, the home of Governor Shelby, where he had been invited to break his travel.

All that nigh he rode and at sunrise was far away. Pausing on a height and turning his horse's head, he sat a long time motion-less as a statue. Then he struck his feet into its flank and all that day rode back again.

The sun was striking the tree-tops as he neared the clearing. He could see her across the garden. She sat quite still, her face turned toward the horizon. Against her breast, opened but forgotten, lay a book. He could recognize it. By that story she had judged him and wished to guide him. The smile smote his eyes like the hilt of a knight's sword used as a Cross to drive away the Evil One. For he knew the evil purpose with which he had returned.

And so he sat watching her until she rose and walked slowly to the house.

XXII

IT was early autumn when the first letters from him were received over the mountains. All these had relation to Mount Vernon and his business there.

To the Transylvania Library Committee he wrote that the President had mad a liberal subscription for the buying of books and that the Vice-President and other public men would be likely to contribute.

His sonorous, pompous letter to a member of the Democratic Society was much longer and in part as follows:

"When I made know to the President who I was and where I came from, he regarded me with a look at once so stern and so benign, that I felt like one of my school-boys overtaken in some small rascality and was almost of a mind to march straight to a corner of the room and stand with my face to the wall. If he had seized me by the coat collar 'and trounced me well, I should somehow have felt that he had the right. From the conversations that followed I am led to believe that he knows the name of every prominent member of the Democratic Society of Lexington, and that he understands Kentucky affairs with regard to national and international complications as no other living man. While questioning me on the subject, he had the manner of one who, from conscientiousness, would further verify facts which he had already tested. But what impressed me even more than his knowledge was hisjustice; in illustration of which I shall never forget his saying, that the part which Kentucky had taken, or had wished to take, in the Spanish and French conspiracies had caused him greater solicitude than any other single event since the foundation of the National Government; but that nowhere else in America had the struggle for immediate self-government been so necessary and so difficult, and that nowhere else were the mistakes of patriotic and able men more natural or more to be judged with mildness.

"I think I can quote his very words when he spoke of the foolish jealousies and heartburnings, due to misrepresentations, that have influenced Kentucky against the East as a section and against the Government as favouring it: 'The West derives from the East supplies requisite to its growth and comfort; and what is perhaps of still greater consequence, it must of necessity owe the secure enjoyment of indispensable outlets for its own production to the weight, influence, and future maritime strength of the Atlantic side of the Union, directed by an indissoluble community of interest, as One Nation.'

"Memorable to me likewise was the language in which he proceeded to show that this was true:

"'The inhabitants of our Western country have lately had a useful lesson on this head. They have seen in the negotiations by the Executive, and in the unanimous ratification by the Senate of the treaty with Spain, and in the universal satisfaction of that event throughout the United States, a decisive proof how unfounded were the suspicions propagated among them of a policy in the General Government and in the Atlantic States unfriendly to their interests in regard to the Mississippi. . . . Will they not henceforth be deaf to those advisers, if such there are, who would sever them from their Brethren and connect them with Aliens?'

"I am frank to declare that, having enjoyed the high privilege of these interviews with the President and been brought to judge rightly what through ignorance I had judged amiss, I feel myself in honour bound to renounce my past political convictions and to resign my membership in the Lexington Democratic Society. Nor shall I join the Democratic Society of Philadelphia, as had been my ardent purpose; and it will not be possible for me on reaching that city to act as the emissary of the Kentucky Clubs. But I shall lay before the Society the despatches of which I am the bearer. And will you lay before yours the papers herewith enclosed, containing my formal resignation with the grounds thereof carefully stated?"

To Mrs. Falconer he wrote bouyantly:

"I have crossed the Kentucky Alps, seen the American Caesar, carried away some of his gold. I came, I saw, I overcame. How do you think I met the President? I was riding toward Mount Vernon one quiet sunny afternoon and unexpectedly came upon an old gentleman who was putting up some bars that opened into a wheat-filed by the roadside. He had on long boots, corduroy smalls, a speckled red jacket, blue coat with yellow buttons, and a broad-brimmed hat. He held a hickory switch in his hand. An umbrella and a long staff were attached to his saddle-bow. His limbs were so long, large, and sinewy; his countenance so lofty, masculine, and contemplative; and although he was of a presence so statue-like and venerable that my heart with a great throb cried out, It is Washington!"

"My dear friend," he wrote at the close, "it is of no little worth to me that I should have come to Mount Vernon at this turning-point of my life. I find myself uplifted to a plane of thought and feeling higher than has ever been trod by me. When I began to draw near this place, I seemed to be mounting higher, like a man ascending a mountain; and ever since my arrival there has been this same sense of rising into a still loftier atmosphere, of surveying a vaster horizon, of beholding the juster relations of surrounding objects.

"All this feeling has its origin in my contemplation of the character of the President. You know that when a heavy sleet falls upon the Kentucky forest, the great trees crack and split, or groan and stagger, with branches snapped off or trailing. In adversity it is often so with men. But he is a vast mountain-peak, always calm, always lofty, always resting upon a base that nothing can shake; never higher, never lower, never changing; from every quarter of the earth storms have rushed in and beaten upon him; but they have passed; he is as he was. The heavens have emptied their sleets and snows on his head, - these have made him look only purer, only the more sublime.

"From the spectacle of this great man thus bearing the great burdens of his great life, a new standard of what is possible to human nature has been raised within me. I have seen with my own eyes a man whom the adverse forces of the world have not been able to wreck - a lover of perfection, who has so wrought it out in his character that to know him is to be awed into

James Lane Allen

reverence of his virtues. I shall go away from him with nobler hopes of what a man may do and be.

"It is to you soley that I owe the honour of having enjoyed the personal consideration of the President. His reception of me had been in the highest degree ceremonious and distant; but upon my mentioning the names of father and brother, his manner grew warm: I had touched that trait of affectionate faithfulness with which he has always held on to every tie of kin and friendship. That your father should have fought against him and your brother under him made no difference in his memory. He had many questions to ask regarding you - your happiness, your family - to some of which I could return the answers that gave him pleasure or left him thoughtful. Upon my setting out from Mount Vernon, his last words made me the bearer of his message to you, the child of an old comrade and the sister or a gallant young soldier."

Beyond this there was nothing personal in his letter and nothing as to his return.

When she next heard, he was in Philadelphia, giving his attention to the choosing and shipment of the books. One piece of news, imparted in perfect calmness by him, occasioned her acute disappointment. His expectation of coming into possession of some ten thousand dollars had not quite been realized. An appeal had been taken and the case was yet pending. He was pleased neither with the good faith nor with the good sense of the counsel engaged; and he would remain on the spot himself during the trial. He added that he was lodging with a pleasant family. Then followed the long winter during which all communication between the frontier and the seaboard was interrupted. When spring returned at last and the earliest travel was resumed, other letters came, announcing that the case had gone against him, and that he had nothing.

She sold at once all the new linen that had been woven, got together all the money she otherwise could and despatched it with Major Falconer's consent, begging him to make use of it for the sake of their friendship - not to be foolish and proud: there were lawyers' fees it could help to pay, or other plain practical needs it might cover. But when the post-rider returned, he brought it all back with a letter of gratitude: only, he couldn't accept it. And the messenger had been warned not to let it be known that he was in prison for debt on account of these same suit expenses; for having from the first formed a low opinion of his counsel's honour and ability and having later expressed this opinion at the door of the court-room with a good deal of fire and a good deal of contempt, and being furthermore unable and unwilling to pay the exorbitant fee, he had been promptly clapped into jail by the incensed attorney, as well for his poverty and for his temper and his pride.

In jail he spent that spring and summer and autumn. Then an important turn was given to his history. It seems that among the commissions with which he was charged on leaving Lexington was one from Edward West, the watchmaker and inventor, who some time before, and long before Fulton, had made trial of steam navigation with a small boat on the Town Fork of the Elkhorn, and who desired to have his invention brought before the American Philosophical Society of Philadelphia. He had therefore placed a full description of his steamboat in John's hands with the request that he would enforce this with the testimony of an eye-witness as to its having moved through water. At this time, through Franklin's influence, the Society was keenly interested in the work of inventors, having received also some years previous from Hyacinthe de Magellan two hundred guineas to be used for rewarding the authors of improvements and discoveries. Accordingly it took up the subject of West's invention but desired to hear more regarding the success of the experiment; and so requested John to appear before it at one of its meetings. But upon looking for this obscure John and finding him in jail, the committee were under the necessity of appearing before him. Whereupon, grown interested in him and made acquainted with the ground of his unreasonable imprisonment, some of the members effected his release - by recourse to the attorney with certain well-direct threats that he could easily be put into jail for his own debts. Not only this; but soon afterwards the young Westerner was taken into the law-office of one of these gentlemen, binding himself for a term of years.

It was not until spring that he wrote he humorously of his days in jail; but when it came to telling her of the other matter, the words refused to form themselves before his will or his hand to shape them on the paper. He would do this in the next letter, he said to himself mournfully.

But early that winter Major Falconer had died, and his next letter was but a short hurried reply to one from her, bringing him this intelligence. And before he wrote again, certain grave events had happened that led him still further to defer acquainting her with his new situation, new duties, new plans.

That same spring, then, during which he was entering upon his career in Philadelphia, she too began really to live. And beginning to live, she began to build - inwardly and outwardly; for what is all life but ceaseless inner and outer building?

As the first act, she sold one of the major's military grants, reserving the ample, noble, parklike one on which she had passed existence up to this; and near the cabin she laid the foundations of her house. Not the great ancestral manor-house on the James and yet a seaboard aristocratic Virginia country-place: two story brick with two-story front veranda of Corinthian columns; wide hall, wide stairway; oak wood interior, hand-carved, massive; sliding doors between the large library and large dining-room; great bedrooms, great fireplaces, great brass fenders and fire-dogs, brass locks and keys: full of elegance, spaciousness, comfort, rest.

In every letter she sent him that spring and summer and early autumn, always she had something to tell him about this house, about the room in it built for him, about the negros she had bought, the land she was clearing, the changes and improvements everywhere: as to many things she wanted his advice. That year also she sent back to Virginia for flower-seed and shrub and plants - the same old familiar ones that had grown on her father's lawn, in the garden, about the walls, along the water - some of which had been bought over from England: the flags, the lilies, honeysuckles, calacan-thus, snowdrops, roses - all of them. Speaking of this, she wrote him that of course that most of these would have to be set out that autumn, and little could be done for grounds till the following season; but the house! - it was to be finished before winter set in. In the last of these letters, she ended by saying: "I think I know now the very day you will be coming back. I can hear your horse's feet rustling in the leaves of - I said - October; but I will say November this time."

His replies were unsatisfying. There had been the short, hurried, earnest letter, speaking of Major Falconer's death: that was all right. But since then a vague blinding mist had seemed to lie between her eyes and every page. Something was kept hidden - some new trouble. "I shall understand everything when he comes!" she would say to herself each time. "I can wait." Her buoyancy was irrepressible.

Late that autumn the house was finished - one of those early country-places yet to be seen here and there on the landscape of Kentucky, marking the building era of the aristocratic Virginians and renewing in the wilderness the architecture of the James.

She had taken such delight in furnishing her room: in the great bedstead with its mighty posts, its high tester, its dainty, hiding curtains; such delight in choosing, in bleaching, in weaving the linen for it! And the pillowcases - how expectant they were on the two pillows now set side by side at the head of the bed, with the delicate embroidery in the centre of each! At first she had thought of working her initials within an oval-shaped vine; but one day, her needle suddenly arrested in the air, she had simply worked a rose.

Late one afternoon, when the blue of Indian summer lay on the walls of the forest like a still sweet veil, she came home from a walk in the woods. Her feet had been rustling among the brown leaves and each time she had laughed. At her round white throat she had pinned a scarlet leaf, from an old habit of her girlhood. But was not Kentucky turning into Virginia? Was not womanhood becoming girlhood again? She was still so young - only thirty-eight. She had the right to be bringing in from the woods a bunch of the purple violets of November.

She sat down in her shadowy room before the deep fireplace; where there was such comfort now, such loneliness. In early years at such hours she had like to play. She resolved to get her a spinet. Yes; and she would have myrtle-berry candles instead of tallow, and a slender-legged mahogany table beside which to read again in the Spectator and "Tom Jones." As nearly as she could she would bring back everything that she had been used to in her childhood - was not all life still before her? If he were coming, it must be soon, and she would know what had been keeping him - what it was that had happened. She had walked to meet him so many times already. And the heartless little gusts of wind, starting up among the leaves in the woods, how often they had fooled her ear and left her white and trembling!

The negro boy who had been sent to town on other business and to fetch the mail, soon afterwards knocked and entered. There was a letter from him - a short one and a paper. She read the letter and could not believe her own eyes, could not believe her own mind. Then she opened the paper and read the announcement of it printed there": he was married.

That night in her bedroom - with the great clock measuring out life in the corner - the red logs turning slowly to ashes - the crickets under the bricks of the hearth singing of summer gone - that night, sitting by the candle-stand, where his letter lay opened, in a nightgown white as white samite, she loosened the folds of her heavy lustrous hair - wave upon wave - until the edges that rippled over her forehead rippled down over her knees. With the loosening of her hair somehow had come the loosening of her tears. And with the loosening of her tears came the loosening of her hold upon what she, until this night, had never acknowledged to herself - her love for him, the belief that he had loved her.

The next morning the parson, standing a white, cold shepherd before his chilly wilderness flock, preached a sermon from the text: "I shall go softly all my years." While the heads of the rest were bowed during the last moments of prayer, she rose and slipped out.

"Yes," she said to herself, gathering her veil closely about her face as she alighted at the door of her house and the withered leaves of November were whirled fiercely about her feet, "I shall go softly all my years."

XXIII

AFTER this the years were swept along. Fast came the changes in Kentucky. The prophecy which John Gray had made to his school-children passed to its realization and reality went far beyond it. In waves of migration, hundreds upon hundreds of thousands of settlers of the Anglo-Saxon race hurried into the wilderness and there jostled and shouldered each other in the race passion of soil-owning and home-building; or always farther westward they rushed, pushing the Indian back. Lexington became the chief manufacturing town of the new civilization, thronged by merchants and fur-clad traders; gathered into it were men and women making a society that would have been brilliant in the capitals of the East; at its bar were heard illustrious voices, the echoes of which are not yet dead, are past all dying; the genius of young Jouett found for itself the secret of painting canvases so luminous and true that never since in the history of the State have they been equalled; the Transylvania University arose with lecturers famous enough to be known in Europe: students of law and medicine travelled to it from all parts of the land.

John Gray's school-children grew to be men and women. For the men there were no longer battles to fight in Kentucky, but there were the wars of the Nation; and far away on the widening boundaries of the Republic they conquered or failed and fell; as volunteers with Perry in the victory on Lake Erie; in the awful massacre at the River Raisin; under Harrison at the Thames; in the mud and darkness of the Mississippi at New Orleans, repelling Pakenham's charge with Wellington's veteran, victory-flushed campaigners.

The school-master's friend, the parson, he too had known his more peaceful warfare, having married and become a manifold father. Of a truth it was feared at one period that the parson was running altogether to prayers and daughters. For it was remarked that with each birth, his petitions seemed longer and his voice to rise from behind the chancel with a fresh wail as of one who felt a growing grievance both against himself and the almighty. Howbeit, innocently enough after the appearance of the fifth female infant, one morning he preached the words: "No man knoweth what manner of creature he is"; and was unaware that a sudden smile rippled over the faces of his hearers. But it was not until later on when mother and six were packed into one short pew at morning service, that they became known in a body as the parson's Collect for all Sundays.

Sometimes the little ones were divided and part of them sat in another pew where there was a single occupant - a woman - childless.

"Yes", she had said, "I shall go softly all my years."

The plants she had brought that summer from Virginia had long since become old bushes. The Virginia Creeper had climbed to the tops of the trees. The garden, though in the same spot, was another place now, with vine-heavy arbours and sodden walks running between borders of flowers and vegetables - daffodils and thyme - in the quaint Virginia fashion. There was a lawn covered as the ancestral one had been with the feathery grass of England. There was a park where the deer remained at home in their wilderness.

Crowning this landscape of comfort and good taste, stood the house. Often of nights when its roof lay deep under snow and the eaves were bearded with hoary icicles, there were candles twinkling at every window and the sounds of music and dancing in the parlours. Once a year there was a great venison supper in the dining-room, draped with holly and mistletoe. On Christmas eve man a child's sock or stocking was hung - no one knew when or by whom - around the shadowy chimney-seat of her room; and every Christmas morning the little negros from the cabins knew to whom each of these belonged. In spring, parties of young girls and youths came out from town for fishing parties and picknicked in the lawn amid the dandelions and under the song of the blackbird; during the summer, for days at a time, other gay company filled the house; of autumns there were nutting parties in the russet woods. Other guests also, not young, not gay. Aaron Burr was entertained there; there met for counsel the foremost Western leaders in his magnificent conspiracy. More than one great man of his day, middle-aged, unmarried, began his visits, returned oftener for awhile - always alone - and one day drove away disappointed.

Through seasons and changes she had gone softly: never retreating from life but drawing about her as closely as she could its ties, its sympathies, it duties: in

James Lane Allen

all things a character of the finest equipois, the truest moderation.

But these are women of the world - some of us men may have discerned one of them in the sweep of our experiences - to whom the joy and the sorrow come alike with quietness. For them there is neither the cry of sudden delight nor the cry of sudden anguish. Gazing deep into their eyes, we are reminded of the light of dim churches; hearing their voices, we dream of some minstrel whose murmurs reach us imperfectly through his fortress wall; beholding the sweetness of their faces, we are touched as by the appeal of the mute flowers; merely meeting them in the street, we recall the long-vanished image of the Divine Goodess. They are the women who have missed happiness and who know it, but having failed of affection, give themselves to duty. And so life never rises high and close about them as about one who stands waist-deep in a wheat-field, gathering at will either its poppies or its sheaves; it flows forever away as from one who pauses waist-deep in a stream and hearkens rather to the rush of all things toward the eternal deeps. It was into the company of theses quieter pilgrims that she had passed: she had missed happiness twice.

Her beauty had never failed. Nature had fought hard in her for all things; and to the last youth of her womanhood it burned like an autumn rose which some morning we may have found on the lawn under a dew that is turning to ice. But when youth was gone, in the following years her face began to reflect the freshness of Easter lilies. For prayer will in time make the human countenance its own divinest alter; years upon years of true thoughts, like ceaseless music shut up within, will vibrate along the nerves of expression until the lines of the living instrument are drawn into correspondence, and the harmony of visible form matches the unheard harmonies of the mind. It was about this time also that there fell upon her hair the earliest rays of the light which is the dawn of Eternal Morning.

She had never ceased to watch his career as part of her very life. Time was powerless to remove him farther from her than destiny had removed him long before: it was always yesterday; the whole past with him seemed caught upon the clearest mirror just at her back. Once or twice a year she received a letter, books, papers, something; she had been kept informed of the birth of his children. From other sources - his letters to the parson, traders between Philadelphia and the West - she knew other things: he had risen in the world, was a judge, often leading counsel in great cases, was almost a great man. She planted her pride, her gratitude, her happiness, on this new soil: they were the few seed that a woman in the final years will sow in a window-box and cover the window-pane and watch and water and wake and think of in the night - she who was used once to range the fields.

But never from the first to last had she received a letter from him that was transparent; the mystery stayed unlifted; she had to accept the constancy of his friendship without its confidence. Question or chiding of course there never was from her; inborn refinement alone would have kept her from curiosity or prying; but she could not put away the conviction that the concealment which he steadily adhered to was either delicately connected with his marriage or registered but too plainly some downward change in himself. Which was it, or was it both? Had he too missed happiness? Missed it as she had - by a union with a

James Lane Allen

perfectly commonplace, plodding, unimaginative, unsympathetic, unrefined nature? And was it a mercy to be able to remember him, not to know him?

These thoughts filled her so often, so often! For into the busiest life - the life that toils to shut out thought - the inevitable leisure will come; and with the leisure will return the dreaded emptiness, the loneliness, the never stifled need of sympathy, affection, companion-ship - for that world of two outside of which every other human being is a stranger. And it was he who entered into all these hours of hers as by a right that she had neither the heart nor the strength to question.

For behind everything else there was one thing more - deeper than anything else, dearer, more sacred; the feeling she would never surrender that for a while at least he had cared more for her than he had ever realized.

One mild afternoon of autumn she was walking with quiet dignity around her garden. She had just come from town where she had given to Jouett the last sitting of her portrait, and she was richly dressed in the satin gown and cap of lace which those who see the picture nowadays will remember. The finishing of it had saddened her a little; she meant to leave it to him; and she wondered whether, when he looked into the eyes of this portrait, he would at last understand": she had tried to tell him the truth; it was the truth that Jouett painted.

Thus she was thinking of the past as usual; and once she paused in the very spot where one sweet afternoon of May long ago he had leaned over the fence, holding in his hand his big black had decorated with a Jacobin cockade, and had asked her consent to marry Amy. Was not yonder the very maple, in the shade of which he and she sat some weeks later while she had talked with him about the ideals of life? She laughed, but she touched her handkerchief to her eyes as she turned to pass on. Then she stopped abruptly.

Coming down the garden walk toward her with a light rapid step, his head in the air, a smile on his fresh noble face, an earnest look in his gray eyes, was a tall young fellow of some eighteen years. A few feet off he lifted his hat with a free, gallant air, uncovering a head of dark-red hair, closely curling.

"I beg your pardon, madam," he said, in a voice that fell on her ears like music long remembered. "Is this Mrs. Falconer?"

"Yes," she replied, beginning to tremble, "I am Mrs. Falconer."

"Then I should like to introduce myself to you, dearest madam. I am John Gray, the son of your old friend, and my father sends me to you to stay with you if you will let me. And he desires me to deliver this letter."

"John Gray!" she cried, running forward and searching his face. "You John Gray! You! Take off your hat!" For a moment she looked at his forehead and his hair; her eyes became blinded with tears. She threw her arms around his neck with a sob and covered his face with kisses.

"Madam," said the young fellow, stooping to pick up his hat, and laughing outright at his own blushes and confusion, " I don't wonder that my father thinks so much of you!"

"I never did that to your father!" she retorted. Beneath the wrinkled ivory of her skin a tinge of faintest pink appeared and disappeared.

Half and hour later she was sitting at a western window. Young John Gray had gone to the library to write to his father and mother, announcing his arrival; and in her lap lay his father's letter which with tremulous fingers she was now wiping her spectacles to read. In all these years she had never allowed herself to think of her John Gray as having grown older; she saw him still young, as when he used to lean over the garden fence. But now the presence of this son had the effect of suddenly pushing the father far on into life; and her heart ached with this first realization that he too must have passed the climbing-point and have set his feet on the shaded downward slope that leads to the quiet valley.

His letter began lightly:

"I send John to you with the wish that you will be to the son the same inspiring soul you once were to the father. You will find him headstrong and with great notions of what he is to be in the world. But he is warm-hearted and clean-hearted. Let him do for you the things I used to do; let him hold the yarn on his arms for you to wind off, and read to you your favourite novels; he is a good reader for a young fellow. And will you get out your spinning-wheel some night when the logs are in roaring in the fireplace and let him hear its music? Will you some time with your hands make him a johnny-cake on a new ash shingle? I want him to know a woman who can do all things and still be a great lady. And lay upon him all the burdens that in any way you can, so that he shall not think too much of what he may some day do in life, but, of what he is actually doing. We get great reports of the Transylvania University, of the bar of Lexington, of the civilization that I foresaw would spring up in Kentucky; and I send John to you with the wish that he hear lectures and afterward go into the office of some one whom I shall name, and finally marry and settle there for life. You recall this as the wish of my own; through John shall be done what I could not do. You see how stubborn I am! I have given him the names of my school-children. He is to find out those of them who still live there, and to tell me of those who have passed away or been scattered.

"I do not know; but if at the end of life I should be left alone here, perhaps I shall make my way back to Kentucky to John, as the old tree falls beside the young one."

From this point the tone of the letter changed.

"And now I am going to open to you what no other eye has ever seen, must ever see - one page in the book of my life."

When she reached these words with a contraction of the heart and a loud throbbing of the pulses in her ears, she got up and locked the letter in her bureau. Then, commanding herself, she went to the dining-room, and with her own hands prepared the supper table; got our her finest linen, glass, silver; had the sconces lighted, extra candelabra brought in; gave orders for especial dishes to be cooked; and when everything was served, seated her guest at the foot of the table and let him preside as though it were his old rightful place. Ah, how like his father he was! Several times when the father's name was mentioned, he quite choked up with tears.

At an early hour he sought rest from the fatigue of travel. She was left alone. The house was quiet. She summoned the negro girl who slept on the floor in her room and who was always with her of evenings:

"You can go to the cabin till bedtime. And when you come in, don't make any noise. And don't speak to me. I shall be asleep."

Then seating herself beside the little candle stand which mercifully for her had had shed its light on so many books in the great lonely bedchamber, she re-read those last words:

"And now I am going to open to you what no other eye has ever seen, must ever see - one page in the book of my life:

"Can you remember the summer I left Kentucky? On reaching Philadelphia I called on a certain family consisting, as I afterwards ascertained, of father, mother, and daughter; and being in search of lodgings, I was asked to become a member of their household. This offer was embraced the more eagerly because I was sick for a home that summer and in need of some kind soul to lean on in my weakness. I had indeed been led for these reasons to seek their acquaintance - the father and mother having known my own parents even before I met them. You will thus understand how natural a haven with my loneliness and amid such memories this house became to me, and upon what grounds I stood in my association with its members from the beginning.

"When the lawsuit went against me and I was wrongfully thrown into jail for debt, their faithful interest only deepened. Very poor themselves, they would yet have make any sacrifice in my behalf. During the months of my imprisonment they were often with me, bringing every comfort and brightening the dulness of many an hour.

"Upon my release I returned gladly to their joyous household, welcomed I could not say with what joyous affection. Soon afterwards I found a position in the office of a law firm and got my start in life.

"And now I cross the path of some things that cannot be written. But you who know what my life and character had been will nobly understand: remember your last words to me.

"One day I offered my hand to the daughter. I told her the whole truth: that there was some one else - not free; that no one could take the place of this other was filling at the moment, and would always fill. Nevertheless, if she would accept me on these conditions, everything that it was in my power to promise she could have.

"She said that in time she would win the rest.

"A few weeks later that letter came from you, bringing the intelligence that changed everything. (Do you remember my reply? I seem only this moment to have dropped the pen.) As soon as I could control myself, I told her that now you were free, that it was but justice and kindness alike to her and to me that I should give here the chance to reconsider the engagement. A week passed, I went again. I warned her how different the situation had become. I could promise less than before - I could not say how little. A month later I went again.

"Ah, well - that is all!

"The summer after my marriage I travelled to Virginia regarding a landsuit. One day I rode far out of my course into the path of the country where you lived. I remained some days strolling over the silent woods and fields, noting the bushes on the lawn, such as you had carried over into Kentucky, hunting out the quiet nooks where you were used to read in your girlhood. Those long, sweet, sacred summer days alone with you there before you were married! O Jessica! Jessica! Jessica! Jessica! And to this day the sight of peach blossoms in the spring - the rustle of autumn leaves under my feet! Can you recall the lines of Malory? 'Men and women could love together seven years, and then was love truth and faithfulness.' How many more than seven have I loved you! - you who never gave me anything but friendship, but who would in time, I hope, have given me everything if I had come back. Ah, I did come back! Many a time even now as soon as I have hurried through the joyous gateways of sleep, I come back over the mountains to you as naturally as though there had been no years to separate and to age. Let me tell you all this! My very life would be incomplete without it! I owed something to you long before I owed anything to another: a duty can never set aside a duty. And as to what I have owed you since, it becomes more and more the noblest earthly that I shall ever leave unpaid. I did not know you perfectly when we parted: I was too young, too ignorant of the world, too ignorant of many women. A man must have touched their coarseness in order to appreciate their refinement; have been wounded by untruthfulness to understand their delicate honour; he must have been driven to turn his eyes mercifully away from their stain before he can ever look with all the reverence and gratitude of his heart and soul upon their brows of chastity.

"But of my life otherwise. I take it fir granted that you would know where I stand, what I have become, whether I have kept faith with the ideals of my youth.

"I have succeeded, perhaps reached now what men call the highest point of their worldly prosperity, made good my resolve that no human power should defeat me. All that Macbeth had not I have: a quiet throne of my own, children, wife, troops of friends, duties, honours, ease. There have been times when with natural misgiving lest I had wandered too far these many summers on a sea of glory, I have prepared for myself the lament of Wolsey on his fall: yet ill fortune had not overwhelmed me or mine.

"All this prosperity, as the mere fruit of my toil, has been less easy than for many. I may not boast the Apostle that I have fought a good fight, but I can say that I fought a hard one. The fight will always be hard for any man who undertakes to conquer life with the few simple weapons I have used and who will accept victory only upon such terms as I have demanded. For be my success small or great, it has been won without inner compromise or other form of self-abasement. No man can look me in the eyes and say I ever wronged him for my own profit; none may charge that I have

James Lane Allen

smiled on him in order to use him, or call him my friend that I might make him do for me the work of a servant.

"Do not imagine I fail to realize that I have added my full share to the general evil of the world: in part unconsciously, in part against my conscious will. It is the knowledge of this influence of imperfection forever flowing from myself to all others that has taught me charity with all the wrongs that flow from others toward me. As I have clung to myself despite the evil, so I have clung to the world despite all the evil that is in the world. To lose faith in men, not humanity; to see justice go down and not believe in the triumph of injustice; for every wrong that you weakly deal another or another deals you to love more and more the fairness and beauty of what is right; and so to turn with ever-increasing love from the imperfection that is in us all to the Perfection that is above us all - the perfection that is God: this is one of the ideals of actual duty that you once said were to be as candles in my hand. Many a time this candle has gone out; but as quickly as I could snatch any torch - with your sacred name on my lips - it has been relighted.

"My candles are all beginning to burn low now. For as we advance far on into life, one by one our duties end, one by one the lights go out. Not much ahead of me now must lurk the great mortal changes, coming always nearer, always faster. As they approach, I look less to my candles, more toward my candles, more toward my lighthouses - those distant unfailing beacons that cast their rays over the stormy sea of this life from the calm ocean of the Infinate. I know this: that if I should live to be an old man, my duties ended and my candles gone, it is these that will shine in upon me in that vacant darkness. And I have this belief: that if we did but recognize them aright, these ideals at the close of life would become one with the ideals of youth. We lost them as we left mortal youth behind; we regain them as we enter upon youth immortal.

"If I have kept unbroken faith with any of mine, thank you. And thank God!"

Choose from Thousands of 1stWorldLibrary Classics By

Adolphus WilliamWard
Aesop
Agatha Christie
Alexander Aaronsohn
Alexander Kielland
Alexandre Dumas
Alfred Gatty
Alfred Ollivant
Alice Duer Miller
Alice Turner Curtis
Alice Dunbar
Ambrose Bierce
Amelia E. Barr
Andrew Lang
Andrew McFarland Davis
Anna Sewell
Annie Besant
Annie Hamilton Donnell
Annie Payson Call
Anton Chekhov
Arnold Bennett
Arthur Conan Doyle
Arthur Ransome
Atticus
B. M. Bower
Basil King
Bayard Taylor
Ben Macomber
Booth Tarkington
Bram Stoker
C. Collodi
C. E. Orr
C. M. Ingleby
Carolyn Wells
Catherine Parr Traill
Charles A. Eastman
Charles Dickens
Charles Dudley Warner
Charles Farrar Browne
Charles Ives
Charles Kingsley
Charles Lathrop Pack
Charles Whibley
Charles Willing Beale
Charlotte M. Braeme
Charlotte M.Yonge
Clair W. Hayes
Clarence Day Jr.
Clarence E. Mulford

Clemence Housman
Confucius
Cornelis DeWitt Wilcox
Cyril Burleigh
D. H. Lawrence
Daniel Defoe
David Garnett
Don Carlos Janes
Donald Keyhole
Dorothy Kilner
Dougan Clark
E. Nesbit
E.P.Roe
E. Phillips Oppenheim
Edgar Allan Poe
Edgar Rice Burroughs
Edith Wharton
Edward J. O'Biren
John Cournos
Edwin L. Arnold
Eleanor Atkins
Elizabeth Cleghorn
Gaskell
Elizabeth Von Arnim
Ellem Key
Emily Dickinson
Erasmus W. Jones
Ernie Howard Pie
Ethel Turner
Ethel Watts Mumford
Eugenie Foa
Eugene Wood
Evelyn Everett-Green
Everard Cotes
F. J. Cross
Federick Austin Ogg
Ferdinand Ossendowski
Francis Bacon
Francis Darwin
Frances Hodgson Burnett
Frank Gee Patchin
Frank Harris
Frank Jewett Mather
Frank L. Packard
Frederick Trevor Hill
Frederick Winslow Taylor
Friedrich Kerst
Friedrich Nietzsche
Fyodor Dostoyevsky

Gabrielle E. Jackson
Garrett P. Serviss
Gaston Leroux
George Ade
Geroge Bernard Shaw
George Ebers
George Eliot
George MacDonald
George Orwell
George Tucker
George W. Cable
George Wharton James
Gertrude Atherton
Grace E. King
Grant Allen
Guillermo A. Sherwell
Gulielma Zollinger
Gustav Flaubert
H. A. Cody
H. B. Irving
H. G. Wells
H. H. Munro
H. Irving Hancock
H. Rider Haggard
H. W. C. Davis
Hamilton Wright Mabie
Hans Christian Andersen
Harold Avery
Harold McGrath
Harriet Beecher Stowe
Harry Houidini
Helent Hunt Jackson
Helen Nicolay
Hendy David Thoreau
Henrik Ibsen
Henry Adams
Henry Ford
Henry Frost
Henry James
Henry Jones Ford
Henry Seton Merriman
Henry Wadsworth
Longfellow
Henry W Longfellow
Herbert A. Giles
Herbert N. Casson
Herman Hesse
Homer
Honore De Balzac

Horace Walpole
Horatio Alger, Jr.
Howard Pyle
Howard R. Garis
Hugh Lofting
Hugh Walpole
Humphry Ward
Ian Maclaren
Israel Abrahams
J.G.Austin
J. Henri Fabre
J. M. Barrie
J. Macdonald Oxley
J. S. Knowles
J. Storer Clouston
Jack London
Jacob Abbott
James Allen
James Lane Allen
James Andrews
James Baldwin
James DeMille
James Joyce
James Oliver Curwood
James Oppenheim
James Otis
Jane Austen
Jens Peter Jacobsen
Jerome K. Jerome
John Burroughs
John F. Kennedy
John Gay
John Glasworthy
John Habberton
John Joy Bell
John Milton
John Philip Sousa
Jonathan Swift
Joseph Carey
Joseph Conrad
Joseph Jacobs
Julian Hawthrone
Julies Vernes
Justin Huntly McCarthy
Kakuzo Okakura
Kenneth Grahame
Kate Langley Bosher
L. A. Abbot
L. T. Meade
L. Frank Baum
Laura Lee Hope

Laurence Housman
Leo Tolstoy
Leonid Andreyev
Lewis Carroll
Lilian Bell
Lloyd Osbourne
Louis Tracy
Louisa May Alcott
Lucy Fitch Perkins
Lucy Maud Montgomery
Lydia Miller Middleton
Lyndon Orr
M. H. Adams
Margaret E. Sangster
Margaret Vandercook
Maria Edgeworth
Maria Thompson Daviess
Mariano Azuela
Marion Polk Angellotti
Mark Overton
Mark Twain
Mary Austin
Mary Cole
Mary Rowlandson
Mary Wollstonecraft
Shelley
Max Beerbohm
Myra Kelly
Nathaniel Hawthrone
O. F. Walton
Oscar Wilde
Owen Johnson
P.G.Wodehouse
Paul and Mable Thorn
Paul G. Tomlinson
Paul Severing
Peter B. Kyne
Plato
R. Derby Holmes
R. L. Stevenson
Rabindranath Tagore
Rahul Alvares
Ralph Waldo Emmerson
Rene Descartes
Rex E. Beach
Richard Harding Davis
Richard Jefferies
Robert Barr
Robert Frost
Robert Gordon Anderson
Robert L. Drake

Robert Lansing
Robert Michael Ballantyne
Robert W. Chambers
Rosa Nouchette Carey
Ross Kay
Rudyard Kipling
Samuel B. Allison
Samuel Hopkins Adams
Sarah Bernhardt
Selma Lagerlof
Sherwood Anderson
Sigmund Freud
Standish O'Grady
Stanley Weyman
Stella Benson
Stephen Crane
Stewart Edward White
Stijn Streuvels
Swami Abhedananda
Swami Parmananda
T. S. Ackland
The Princess Der Ling
Thomas A. Janvier
Thomas A Kempis
Thomas Anderton
Thomas Bailey Aldrich
Thomas Bulfinch
Thomas De Quincey
Thomas H. Huxley
Thomas Hardy
Thomas More
Thornton W. Burgess
U. S. Grant
Valentine Williams
Victor Appleton
Virginia Woolf
Walter Scott
Washington Irving
Wilbur Lawton
Wilkie Collins
Willa Cather
Willard F. Baker
William Makepeace
Thackeray
William W. Walter
Winston Churchill
Yei Theodora Ozaki
Young E. Allison
Zane Grey